ALLURED BY HER

CHELSEA M. CAMERON

About Allured By Her

I never looked forward to coming into work at the Common Grounds coffee shop and seeing Tenley Hill sitting at her usual table with her laptop. The most popular girl from high school always seemed to harass me and try to get a free latte and was more infuriatingly pretty than ever.

Then one day she comes in and she's a total wreck. I make the massive mistake of asking her what's wrong. Turns out her boyfriend dumped her and all wants to do is try and get him back. Tenley pours her heart out to me and, for the first time, I see her as a person and not just the woman who annoys me every day. That moment of weakness causes me to agree to do something I never would have done under normal circumstances: date her. Well, pretend to date her. In public, wherever her ex will see us. She tells me it's fine, because she doesn't even like women so there will be no messy complications. I panic and tell her I'm straight too.

At first I hate the role of being a fake girlfriend, but soon I find myself flirting with Tenley and dreaming of her kisses. She's nothing like how I expected and before I know it, I'm falling for my heterosexual fake girlfriend and I have absolutely no idea what the hell I'm going to do about it.

Chapter One

"I ordered an iced macchiato, and this was hot," a voice said behind me. I'd been washing dishes in the sink and I had to grip it for a second before plastering a smile on my face and turning around.

"Tenley. You ordered a hot one. I know. I was the one who took your order," I said, trying to keep my voice even. I had a lot of regulars at the Common Grounds Coffee Shop, but Tenley Hill was by far the most irritating. At least once or twice a week, she came up to the counter and pretended that she'd gotten the wrong order in an effort to try and scam a free coffee out of us. I'd asked my boss, Liam, to ban her from the shop, but he said it wasn't a big deal and she did spend a lot of time and money when she wasn't scamming us. Tenley was here at least three or four days a week for full days with her laptop. She did a lot of typing, but I had never asked her what the hell she was doing all those hours. I didn't care and I didn't want to know.

"Oh come on," Tenley said, leaning on the counter and letting her honey-blonde hair fall over her shoulder. "I *really* need it."

If I didn't know better, I would have said she was trying to flirt, but Tenley Hill would never flirt with someone like me. Girls like me didn't get flirted with by cheerleading-captain prom-queens.

She rolled her eyes. "Okay, fine, give me an iced caramel macchiato. *Extra* caramel."

"Coming right up," I chirped in a fake voice. Tenley and I had gone to high school together and while she might not have given me the time of day then, everyone knew who she was, and they still did around here. Tenley Hill could have anything she wanted, and I was not on that list. Besides, she had a sexy boyfriend that she talked to—often and loudly on her phone. No shocker that he'd been the captain of the basketball and baseball teams. It was a match made in high school heaven. Ugh.

I did my best to put Tenley out of my mind, which wasn't hard, since my job was so fast paced. Most days I barely got a minute to sit down, let alone think.

"She being her charming self?" my coworker and friend Lark asked, nudging my shoulder with hers.

"Always," I said, rolling my eyes. "Can you grab me some more almond milk from the back?"

"Sure," she said, heading to the storage room. I made a few lattes and iced coffees and heated up scones and muffins before she made it back. "Sorry, Liam grabbed me for a second."

"It's okay," I said, taking the almond milk from her so I could froth it into a latte. Lark and I moved in tandem to make everyone in line happy, sliding by each other with the ease of practice. Sometimes our boss, Liam, said it looked like we were dancing. Having chemistry with your coworkers was so important when you were working in a confined space. Lark and I were a great fit.

There was a brief lull that let us take a breath and catch up on things we couldn't do when we were busy.

"No, Shane, I do *not* want to go house hunting with your mother," a sharp voice said, cutting through the soft jazz music that played all day and wormed its way into my brain even when I wasn't at work.

Lark and I shared a look. Tenley was fighting with her perfect boyfriend for the second time this week.

"I should not be enjoying this, but I am," I said to Lark as Tenley continued to argue with Shane. Several other customers shot her dirty looks, but Tenley was oblivious.

"Me too," she said. "I feel like I need popcorn." She pulled out her phone.

"You're not filming her, are you?" I asked.

"No, I'm sending a play-by-play to Sydney. She loves other people's drama," Lark said.

"I should probably tell you that management would frown upon you doing that, but I'm not going to," I said as Tenley continued to talk to Shane and gesture with her free hand. Things were not going well.

"Fine, Shane, that's just *fine*," she said, her voice in that deadly soft tone that just about anyone would recognize. She hung up and set her phone down on the table.

Everyone in the shop was staring at her, but she didn't seem to be bothered. Tenley never seemed bothered by anything that I could tell.

She just went back to typing on her laptop, but her jaw was clenched tight.

"Okay," Lark said with a sigh, pushing back from the counter she'd been leaning on. "Drama over. For now."

"Yeah," I said, still looking at Tenley. Everyone else lost interest, but I saw her reach up and swipe away a tear before she started typing again.

"I wish I could have been there to see it," Sydney said as Lark made dinner that night. When I'd first moved in, they had insisted that I come over for dinner a few times a week and I'd caved due to the pressure from both of them. Lark was my best friend and Sydney was her girlfriend and it was two against one. Plus, Lark had become a really good cook and I got to sit on the couch and gossip with Sydney and pet their fluffy orange cat, Clementine.

"It wasn't the Fourth of July, but it was still pretty intense," I said. "If I didn't know her, I might have felt sorry for her."

"I barely know her, and I don't feel sorry for her," Sydney said. She'd been a few years ahead of us in school, so she hadn't had the misfortune of dealing with Tenley, but she'd heard enough from me and Lark that she'd formed a correct opinion.

"Oh, they'll make up and she'll be back to messaging him constantly and taking selfies to send him," I said. "People like that don't change."

"Maybe," Sydney said, a thoughtful look on her face. "But I thought the same thing about Honor and look at her now. She's one of my closest friends and I'm going to be in her wedding."

"She's also marrying one of your best friends," I pointed out.

"And she's your girlfriend's sister," Lark called from the kitchen. "So you're obligated to be there."

"My point is," Sydney said, raising her hand. "That I didn't like her at first. I was very much Team No Honor, and then I came around. So maybe Tenley could turn out like that."

"You're being very optimistic right now, and I've got to say, it's really hot," Lark said, gesturing at Sydney with a spatula. Sydney turned her attention to Lark and their eyes locked as heat pulsed between them. That was the risk I ran when eating dinner with them. The sexual energy between them was palpable. Sometimes I imagined putting on one of those HAZMAT suits to protect myself from it.

I wasn't jealous per se. Okay, I was a little bit. I loved Lark and I loved Sydney and I loved seeing them together. But then I went down the hall to my apartment that didn't have a girlfriend or even a cat in it and things got bleak.

True, I had plenty going on in my life. I had my full-time job that I didn't completely hate, and then I had my little side hustle making custom silicone sex toys out of my sister's garage. I'd also joined the book club that met once a month at Mainely Books. I babysat my niece and hung out with my sister. I had friends. That was plenty.

At least, that's what I told myself when the loneliness gnawed at me. Everyone felt that way, even people in love. Being lonely was just a fact of life.

"Dinner's ready," Lark said, bringing me out of my mental funk.

"Great," I said, standing up to go grab my plate.

THE FUNK CONTINUED into the next day as Lark, Liam, and I dealt with the morning rush. I tried to shift my brain to autopilot like I usually did and go by muscle memory, but it wasn't working. I kept dropping things and fucking up drinks, but I couldn't stop, couldn't take a break.

"I don't know what is wrong with me today," I said as I went to remake my third drink that I'd messed up.

"You're just having an off day. Happens to all of us," Lark said, chucking a croissant into the warmer.

I topped the finished drink with whipped cream and took it to the counter, calling out the name on the order. The woman wearing scrubs took it and thanked me as I apologized for the wait.

"No problem at all, you have a nice day," she said with a

smile and my stomach did a little flip because hell, she was cute.

"You're welcome," I stuttered and then had to go deal with the next order. My teeth automatically clenched when I met a set of golden-brown eyes set in a pretty face.

"Large iced lavender vanilla macchiato. *Iced*," she said, as if I hadn't heard her the first time. "Light on the ice, heavy on the whip. Please." She added the last word as an afterthought. To be fair, a lot of people didn't know when to use that word, and Tenley always did, eventually. She had that going for her.

"Coming right up," I said with a sigh.

Tenley flashed me a smile and went back to her table to set up her laptop and I went to make her drink.

"How is she today?" Lark asked.

"No more annoying than usual," I said, grabbing her cup and pumping the syrup into it. I double-checked Tenley's drink before I set it on the pickup counter and called out her name.

She came up to get it with her phone attached to her ear. I pointed to the sign that said that phone calls should be taken outside, as a courtesy, but she ignored me like she did every other time I'd drawn her attention to it.

There was a brief lull a few minutes later so Lark and I leaned on the counters to take a breather.

Tenley was still on the phone, and it didn't look like the conversation was going well. Probably fighting with her boyfriend again. Yawn.

"Lark, do you want to take your break?" Liam said, coming out from the back.

"Yes please," Lark said. "Back in fifteen." She squeezed my shoulder as she passed me to head out to the back and chill out on the picnic table in the tiny employee courtyard. We shared our parking lot with a bank and a car wash, but at least we had our own little area.

"You good?" Liam asked, frowning at me.

"I'm good," I said, stretching my wrists and rolling my shoulders.

Liam didn't seem convinced, but then Tenley came up to the counter again.

"I asked for a lavender vanilla latte, and you definitely forgot the lavender syrup," she said, holding up her cup and shaking it.

"I didn't forget the lavender," I said, crossing my arms.

"Oh, I think you did," Tenley said.

"You know we have a rewards program where you get free refills," Liam said, but we both ignored him. Tenley knew this. I'd tried to get her to sign up at least a thousand times before, but she always refused. I didn't get it. She was in here nearly every day, all day. I should just sign her up against her will.

"Fine," I said, because I didn't have the energy to fight with her today.

"Thank you," Tenley sang.

I growled in annoyance and Liam heard me.

"I know we're nice to her, but if she ever becomes a problem, just let me know. I can step in if I have to."

"Thanks," I said. Liam nodded and went to take care of the next customer.

As far as bosses went, Liam was one of the best. Not only wasn't he a massive asshole, he didn't think any job was beneath him. He let people change their schedules if they had to and didn't hassle anyone for taking a break. Sure, he was beholden to the corporate overlords, but he did what he could to defend his employees and we all appreciated it.

When I'd graduated from college two years ago, I'd had no idea what the fuck to do with my psychology degree since I was so completely burned out on school, so I moved back to Arrowbridge and took the first job that offered me a position and here I was, seven-time employee of the month at Common Grounds Coffee.

Every now and then I glanced up to where Tenley was furiously typing away on her laptop, her fingers flying faster than I knew was possible. She frowned as she stared at the screen during a pause in the action and then muttered softly to herself. Whatever she was doing required a lot of focus. One afternoon, someone had had a seizure at the bank across the parking lot and there had been complete chaos with sirens and lights and everyone trying to figure out what was going on. The entire time, Tenley had been staring at her computer and typing and in her own world. I'd never seen anything like it before.

Tenley nodded to herself and then started typing again as Lark returned from her break.

"Your turn," she said.

"Thank you," I said, heading to the little employee room where we stored our stuff and had a small fridge for our lunch and snacks to grab my water.

The sun was out, so I sat my ass directly under it on the top of the picnic table and just let my brain think about absolutely nothing for a few minutes.

An incoming message on my phone disturbed me a few moments later. I sighed before I checked to find a message from my sister, Ingrid, asking me if I could pick up my niece, Athena, from daycare.

No problem, I'll grab her I responded.

Thank you, I just can't get out of this meeting she sent. Ing worked as a high school guidance counselor, so some sort of crisis was always coming up. Since she was a single parent, I often picked up the slack with Athena. It didn't hurt that Athena was three and probably my favorite person on the planet. When she was born, I'd bought a car seat for my car, which had been a wise purchase.

I set my phone down and tried to soak up my last few

minutes of sun before heading back into the coffee shop to go back to the grind.

"AND WHAT DID we learn today, Miss Athena, my warrior queen?" I asked Athena after I'd strapped her in and we were heading to Ingrid's house.

"I found a bug!" she yelled, raising both her arms as I checked her in the rearview mirror.

"Whoa, that's so cool. What kind of bug?" I asked, almost dreading the answer. Athena was super into insects right now, much to my, and her mother's, bemused horror. You've never lived until you've been dozing on your sister's couch and your niece shoves a live spider right in your face, asking you to name it.

"A pider," Athena said. "Piderman." Ah yes, Peter Parker, her other greatest love.

"Was it a real bug, or was it Spiderman?" I asked.

"Real pider," she said, chattering away. This kid was headed for a career in entomology or comic books and I was 50/50 on which one she'd pick.

Athena helped me carry her backpack into my sister's house and immediately asked for a snack.

"Athena, my love, you know that we're not going to have a snack because we're going to have dinner in a few minutes. Are you really hungry?" I asked, looking down at her.

"I'm hungry *now*," she said, stomping her little foot and knocking herself off-balance. I pressed my lips together so I didn't laugh.

"Okay, let's have a small snack while I make dinner. Does that work for you?" I asked.

"I guess," she said, sounding world-weary.

I gave her one of her bags of toddler snacks and started looking through the fridge for something to throw together.

"What do you think about a cheeseburger bowl?" I asked Athena as she sat on the floor of the kitchen with her snack.

"I like cheese," Athena said.

"So do I," I said, grabbing a container of hamburger.

Ingrid arrived home as I was chopping veggies and Athena was on the couch singing along with her favorite kid's streaming show.

"Mama!" Athena said, running across the floor to throw herself at her mother's legs.

"Hey, baby, I missed you today," Ingrid said, dropping her bags and picking up her daughter and giving her kisses all over her face as she giggled.

"Dinner is almost ready," I said as she carried Athena into the kitchen.

"Thanks, I really appreciate it," she said, stroking Athena's hair from her face. It always struck me as funny that the red hair gene had skipped Ingrid but had hit me and her daughter so people assumed she was mine all the time. I often joked that the sperm donor she'd picked must have had the gene in his family, too.

"All in a day's work as an auntie," I said.

"Mama, I need to pee!" Athena announced.

"Okay, why don't you go and yell if you need some help. Don't forget to flush and wash your hands," Ingrid said, and Athena dashed off. She was potty trained. Mostly.

"Rough day?" I asked as Ingrid pulled herself up to sit on the counter.

"Teenagers are going through it, I swear. You could not pay me to go back to those years," she said, rubbing her face.

"Amen to that," I said putting the knife down. "We're ready here if you want to make yourself a bowl."

Ingrid got down from the counter and gave me a hug. "You are the best sister, I swear."

"I'm your only sister," I pointed out.

"Still, you're the best."

"I try," I said as she pulled out the bowls.

I WAS tired when I got home from dinner with my sister and my niece, but I had a package waiting outside my door that I was very excited about. It was the mold for my newest sex toy design. I unlocked my door as fast as I could and ripped into the box, pulling the mold out. You never really knew what the toys would look like until you made one, but this one I was pretty proud of.

I'd started out making very classic shapes but had gotten more and more requests for toys that looked like dragons or tentacles or wolves or horses, or that were inspired from romance books. While I still did my standard toys because they sold, I was adding more and more fun and silly creations. Right now, my sister was the only one who knew about my side hustle. Not even Lark knew.

It wasn't that I was ashamed of it, I just…didn't want people to be weird or creepy. The messages I'd get through my website and social media for the business could be a bit much, and even though I knew Lark would be chill about it, I just hadn't told her yet.

This weekend I was definitely going to take this new mold for a spin and make a practice toy. Very often my testing process led to testing the products myself, which was always fun and informative. I was my own quality control team.

"I love research and development," I said, stroking the mold and then setting it by the door. Since I used chemicals, there was no way to safely make my toys in my apartment, so Ingrid had given me use of her garage.

I thought of my side hustle as "the night shift" because so much of my work had to be done when I wasn't at my day job. Ingrid kept asking me if I wanted to see if I could do my sex toy business full time, but that seemed like way too much stress. I loved the security of having a regular paycheck. Plus, making sex toys was fun, and I was scared that if I relied on it for all my income, the fun would get sucked right out of it. Plus, I wouldn't get to play around with weird shapes and colors that would fail. I wouldn't have enough room for failure.

Sure, I didn't see myself as a lifelong barista, but it worked for me right now. Hell, I'd saved up enough for my own apartment, which was pretty fucking cool. It wasn't a two bed with a terrace, but it was mine and I didn't have to share it with a roommate.

I grabbed my laptop and checked for new orders, printing out the shipping labels and adding them to my stack so I could pack them to ship this weekend. Once that was done, I could make some replacements and then play with my new mold. Storage space was so limited that I could only make a few of each toy at a time. Thankfully, most of my customers were incredibly understanding and I usually threw in a free little mini toy or something fun for them. I'd recently been playing with the idea of doing a monthly subscription box with mystery toys in it for my very loyal customers, but I wasn't sure I had enough space. Ingrid had been so kind to give me her garage, but I was going to need something bigger if I wanted to expand at all.

It was a conundrum that was really starting to stress me out.

I shut my laptop and told myself that it wasn't the end of the world, and that I'd figure it out. Not having enough space to make more sex toys wasn't the biggest problem in the world.

Right now, I needed to watch a trashy show in the tub with some popcorn covered in lots of salt and butter. And ice cream. There was a certain sort of decadence to eating ice cream in a warm bath.

I grabbed my tablet and propped it on the toilet as I filled the tub and selected a bath bomb from the basket beside my bed. Every single holiday when Ingrid had to give me a gift, she always got me bath bombs and I'd built up quite a stockpile. I might not have a million dollars, but I had a basket of bath bombs for whenever I needed them.

Chapter Two

"I'm so glad we have the same shift now," I told Lark the next day during the mid-morning lull.

"I know. What did you do before we worked together all the time?" she asked.

"I had to work with Mindy and it was…a lot." I told her as I snuck a few sips of water.

"You mean Perky?" Lark said with a laugh. Mindy was an absolutely lovely woman who was at least fifteen years older than anyone else who worked here. She'd been a stay-at-home-mom for most of her adult life, and she was extremely excited to have a job outside the house and to get to talk to other adults all day. *Extremely* excited. I'd never met anyone who was that enthusiastic to make macchiatos and warm up croissants all day, but Mindy was sunshine on steroids. You couldn't even be mad at her because she was so completely nice that you felt like an asshole for ever getting annoyed with her. Bless Mindy, but I was glad I didn't have to work with her that much anymore.

"I could be Mindy if you want," Lark said, doing a scarily good impression of Mindy's upbeat voice.

"Please no," I said, covering my ears. "I can't handle it."

Lark just laughed and then pulled out her buzzing phone.

"Ohhh, Everly and Ryan are having a barbecue in a few weeks. You in?" Lark said, looking up at me.

"Yeah, I'm definitely in," I said. Becoming Lark's friend had meant I'd gotten to be part of a whole new friend group. Most of the people I'd been friends with in high school had bailed on Arrowbridge, so it had been strange to come back here and need to make new friends. The people from my class who had stayed weren't the kinds of people I wanted to hang with. Tenley and her boyfriend were Exhibit A.

Everly worked in Arrowbridge at a pottery studio that Sydney ran, and Ryan was the cousin of Lark's sister's fiancée. Sometimes I wanted to make a really confusing tree of all the connections. It was weird to be the only one who didn't have multiple connections to these people, other than being Lark's friend. Maybe it should bother me, but it didn't.

"Nice. It's at Layne's boss's house and Ryan's grilling, so you're in for a lot of good food. Layne is making some so-called life-changing salad and Joy is grabbing dessert from Sweet's. And Everly will surely have a smorgasbord of dips, per usual," Lark said. Everly had become the dip girl at book club every month, so any chance I got to have some made for a good time.

"Should I bring drinks or something?" I asked.

"Yeah, that's what I'm going to do. Just grab some beer or soda or something," she said. "Everything else is covered. One of these days I'll have another big brunch for everyone."

Layne had given Lark unofficial cooking lessons, and Lark loved to show off her skills for an audience.

The door opened and Tenley arrived, a frown on her face already. I dove in front of Lark to go take her order. Tenley being annoyed gave me a little rush. Was it petty? Sure. But it was only fair. Tenley was one of those people that nothing bad had ever happened to. Her path in life had been smooth, and it wasn't fair. Not that my life had been shitty, but still. People like Tenley were just blessed in extra ways. Wealthy parents, well-liked brothers, a car on her sixteenth birthday, trips overseas in the summer, a designer wardrobe, tons of friends, and good grades. When you looked up the word *privileged*, there should be a picture of her face.

Tenley blinked at me as I stood there and waited for her to place her order.

"What can I get for you?" I said a little loudly. She'd been staring off into space, and I noticed that her eyes were red, and she had circles under them.

"Whatever," she finally said. "I just need…something."

I shot a glance at Lark who shrugged.

"You're going to let me just make a random drink for you? I'm not falling for that, Tenley. You'll just drink it and then demand a free one," I said.

She looked down and I'd never seen her so defeated. She wore a set of wrinkled sweats and a baggy t-shirt, and her hair was a tangled mess that she'd crammed into a bun. I'd never seen her so disheveled.

"I just need caffeine, okay? Can you just not hassle me right now? Please?" Her voice cracked on the last word and I truly thought she was going to burst into tears.

What the fuck?

"Yeah, okay, I'll make you something. Uh, are you okay?" I punched in an order for one of our new drinks I thought she might like and a croissant. Instead of handing over her card, Tenley just went to her usual table and dumped her bag on the other chair and sat down.

"She forgot to pay," I told Lark.

"Then go tell her," Lark said, gesturing.

I thought about it, but I didn't want to. As much as I couldn't stand her, I'd feel sympathy for just about anyone in her position. So I punched in the order and did a little finagling to make it free. When her order was ready, instead of slapping it on the counter and calling her name like I usually did, I picked up her order and stepped around the counter to bring it to her.

She looked up when I set it down in front of her.

"What's that?" she asked.

"Your daily croissant and our new macchiato. You'll like it, I promise," I said, feeling weird standing there.

Tenley looked at the drink and then up at me again, blinking in a confused way.

"Now you say 'thank you' and I say 'you're welcome' and then we both go back to work," I said.

"Thank you," she said automatically.

"Uh, you're welcome," I said. I considered asking her if she was okay again, but that was way above my pay grade, and I needed to go help Lark.

I pivoted and headed back behind the counter, glancing back to see Tenley pick up the macchiato and take a tentative sip. She swallowed and then sucked the rest of the drink down before tearing viciously into her croissant. Guess she liked it.

TODAY I WAS off my game and it was all Tenley's fault. She wasn't doing a whole lot of typing, but she was doing a lot of staring off into space. She hadn't come up for another drink, or to pay for the first one I gave her.

"She looks like a social media ad for depression," Lark whispered to me as we made drinks next to each other.

"I know," I said. "I wonder what happened? You'd think if things were that bad she'd stay home."

"Maybe her routine is the only thing she has," Lark said.

"My, that was very introspective of you," I said with a laugh.

"Thank you, thank you," Lark said. "I'm working on it."

An odd sound made us both look up as Tenley stared at her phone and then ran to the bathroom. Luckily for her, it was unoccupied, and she slammed the door shut and locked it.

"Whoa," Lark said, turning to me. "That doesn't sound good at all."

"Seriously," I said, staring at the closed bathroom door. I couldn't hear anything, but my guess was that Tenley was still crying.

"Guess everyone has bad days," Lark said, heading over to give a refill to one of our regulars.

I did my best to ignore the Tenley situation, but it wasn't easy. My eyes kept flicking to the bathroom and then the clock, because she'd been in there for a while.

"Should we check on her?" Lark asked. "Would that be too much?"

"We should at least make sure she's okay," I said. "I'll do it."

"Good luck," Lark said. She could handle the counter on her own for the time it would take me to knock on the door.

I took in a shaky breath before raising my hand and knocking on the door.

"Tenley? Are you okay?" I asked.

Loud sniffing greeted me first. "Go away," she said, her voice thick with tears.

"I will, I just wanted to check on you," I said, trying to hear through the door.

"I'm fine," she growled at me before sniffing loudly again before I heard what sounded like her blowing her nose.

"Okay," I said. "I'll just, uh, be out here if you need anything."

"Go. Away," she said again, and I headed back behind the counter.

"Well?" Lark asked.

"She's just going through something. Asked me to leave her alone." I shrugged and went back to work, but the nagging feeling in the back of my mind wouldn't go away.

∾

TENLEY DIDN'T REAPPEAR for ten more minutes, and when she came out, she was completely wrecked as she shuffled back to her table and sat down.

On an impulse, I made a cup of warm honey chamomile tea and tentatively took it over to her table.

"You should, um, hydrate?" I said and it sounded like a question as I set the cup down on the table and pushed it toward her.

"What?" she said, looking up at me. I couldn't help the little rush of satisfaction as I saw that she wasn't a pretty crier. Tenley truly looked awful, but my pleasure at her misfortune was short-lived.

"I just brought you some tea," I said, pointing to the cup. "And now I'll go back to work." I started inching away from the table, but she shook her head and set her jaw.

"No, sit," she said.

"Huh?" I said.

"Sit down," she said, pointing to the empty chair that didn't have her bag on it.

"Okay?" I said, pulling the chair out. I shot a quick glance at Lark and she gave me a questioning look. I quickly shrugged one shoulder at her and sat down. No idea why I was doing this with Tenley.

A few seconds of awkward silence passed as I wondered how long I had to sit here before I could bolt.

"Shane broke up with me," she said, her voice thick.

"Oh, I'm sorry," I said.

"Are you?" she asked, her voice sharp.

I opened my mouth to answer and then shut it again.

"That's what I thought," Tenley said, sighing and picking up the tea. "I know you don't like me, and you definitely don't like him. You're not exactly subtle about it."

"I'm sorry," I said.

"No, you're not," she said. "It's fine. I don't care." She waved one hand.

"I should get back to work," I said, getting ready to run. Tenley stared out the window.

"I have to get him back," she said softly to herself.

"Well, good luck with that," I said, starting to stand, but one of her hands reached out to stop me.

"Wait. Just hold on a second."

I stopped and sat down again.

"What?" I asked, starting to get fed up.

Tenley licked her lips and I saw a gleam in her eyes that made my stomach drop.

"Shane gets really jealous, you know," she said.

"Uh, no, I didn't, but it's not a surprise," I said. I'd seen the way he'd acted in high school.

"So the way to get him to come back to me is to make him think that he can't have me," she said, and I still didn't know where she was going with this, but her grip on my arm was starting to cut off my circulation.

"Get to the *point*, Tenley," I said.

"Date me," she blurted out.

"What?!" I said, my voice way too loud in the shop. I felt my face go red. "I'm sorry, but *what?*"

"I mean, don't *actually* date me. Just pretend to. Show up at a few parties with me and pretend to be my girlfriend and it will make Shane so jealous that he'll come back to me," she said, and I was about ready to ask her if she had lost her fucking mind.

I started to protest and tell her that under no circumstances would I be doing any of that, but then she shook her head.

"No, no, it's perfect. I'm not gay. I'm only into men, so there's no way that feelings will complicate things. If I asked another guy to do it, he might get confused and I don't need that. I just need to be seen with someone to snap Shane back to the reality that he loves me and that we're meant to be together."

"I've got to be honest, this plan sounds ridiculous. He's not going to buy it," I said.

Tenley shook her head again, and I couldn't help but be transfixed by her. Even as a mess, she was still fucking gorgeous.

"It's not. It's perfect. You're perfect. We're both straight, so it will be easy."

Oh. *OH*.

Tenley thought I was straight. In high school, I had definitely pretended to be straight. I wasn't that great at it, but I faked it enough to blunder my way through four years. Sure, there were other people who were out, but I just hadn't wanted to share that piece of myself. I'd come out in college, and it had been the right decision.

Now, though, I didn't know what to say to her.

An impulse that came from nowhere made me say, "Right. We're both straight."

Once the words were out, I tried to take them back, but I didn't. Instead, I nodded, and Tenley smiled in such a sweet and heartbreaking way that I thought I was going to slide right out of my chair and end up under the table.

"This is going to work," Tenley said. "I'll let you get back to work, but here is my number so we can coordinate." She grabbed the sleeve off the tea I'd brought her and pulled a pen out of her bag. Tenley wrote down her number and handed it to me.

Mechanically, I took it from her and walked back behind the counter to find Lark waiting for me.

"Well? I've been dying of suspense and wishing I could read lips over here," she said. I stared down at the coffee sleeve Tenley had given me.

"I think I just agreed to be her fake girlfriend," I said, and my voice didn't sound like my own.

"You did what?!" Lark said.

A FLOOD of people came in, so I was off the hook for a little bit. Somehow, I was able to shut Tenley away in my mind and just go on barista autopilot until we could breathe again.

Sometime during the rush, Tenley had left, but I couldn't stop glancing at her table, which was probably making the new people sitting there uncomfortable, but I couldn't help myself.

"Okay, now that we have a moment, you did what?" Lark asked me.

"I think I agreed to pretend to be Tenley's girlfriend to make her ex jealous," I said. Those words strung together still didn't make much sense, and I was the one who had agreed to them.

"Mia, why the hell would you do that? You hate her," Lark said, stating the obvious.

"I know," I said, poking at a splotch of something sticky on my shirt.

"Then what the hell were you thinking?" Lark asked.

"Honestly, I have no idea. She seemed so sad and I just kind of…agreed? She gave me her number, so I'll just message her later and say that I changed my mind. What should my excuse be?" I asked.

"I'd go with temporary haunting by a vindictive ghost. I think that's your best bet," Lark said, nodding.

What else was I going to say? It was as good an excuse as any. None of this made any sense. She'd just looked so...sad. Must have triggered some primal impulse in me to help her or something.

It didn't really matter, because I wasn't going through with it. I was going to send her a message later tonight and tell her I was out. She'd have to find someone else to fake date. It wasn't going to be me.

"You coming over for dinner tonight?" Lark asked. "Sydney's cooking and she's making her potsticker soup."

I did love that soup, but I also needed some alone time.

"No, I'm good. I might stop over after for a little bit, though," I said. One of the upsides of living down the hall from each other was that either of us could drop in just about anytime. It was also great for when I'd run out of milk.

"Sounds good. I'll see you later then," Lark said as we both logged into the employee computer to clock out. Mindy had arrived for her evening shift and she was on with Brianna, who was a senior in high school and a really hard worker.

Since I hadn't made any dinner plans, I stopped at the grocery store to grab a rotisserie chicken and a bag of salad so I didn't have to do any actual cooking. Some days after a shift at the coffee shop I just didn't have the energy. All I wanted to do was eat food that required the least prep and sit down. There was simply no getting around the fact that I was on my feet most of the day. No amount of supportive shoes and stretch breaks helped when my body was over it.

After I'd put the groceries away, I tossed the salad in a bowl and topped it with some of the shredded chicken and dumped the package of dressing over the whole thing.

"Oh fuck yeah," I said as I sat on the couch with the bowl and turned on the TV. I had absolutely needed this.

I stabbed a piece of chicken and flipped through my streaming services to see what was new that I might want to watch. Nothing complicated. Something that didn't require my brain to process. I settled on old episodes of a fashion designer show that I'd seen plenty of times before so none of the designs was a surprise, but I could still make snarky comments about anything that I didn't like. No one was here to appreciate my comments, but that didn't matter too much. I shoveled my salad into my mouth and wished I had some kind of machine to rub my feet. I was going to have to get that lacrosse ball and roll them out, but that was too much work right now.

I'd bought some macarons on impulse from the bakery section, so I told myself I was only going to have a few, but soon the container was empty, and I was wondering where they'd gone.

Lark and Sydney probably had something sweet at their apartment but getting it would require me getting up. For half a second I thought about messaging her and asking her to come to me, but she'd been on her feet all day too. Just as I was trying to convince myself to get up, there was a knock at my door.

"It's open," I called.

"Hey, I brought you some brownies. Layne dropped them off with Sydney today and there's no way the two of us can eat this many."

I looked over the back of the couch to see her holding a big plastic container with a lid.

"Have I told you how much I love you recently?" I asked as she came over and sat next to me, setting the container between us.

"It's been a few hours," she said with a sigh, pulling the lid off.

"I don't know what Layne's obsession with brownies is, but I love it," I said, grabbing one of the brownies. It had swirls of marshmallow and was studded with white chocolate chips and graham cracker pieces.

"What even are these?" I asked, taking a bite and almost fainting because it was so good.

"I didn't ask," she said, selecting one for herself and biting into it with a satisfied sound.

"They're always amazing, so I don't think it matters," I said.

"I'm glad Layne finally started making them for more than just Honor, although I'm pretty sure they're going to do a brownie bar or something for the wedding."

"Have they picked a location yet?" I asked.

"Nope. It's a whole thing. Mark keeps saying that he's happy to foot the cost of renting a place for the ceremony and reception as a gift, but Layne keeps trying to fight him on it and I don't know why," she said, leaning back into the couch and pulling one of my blankets over her lap.

"I think Honor is going to tell him to go ahead and put down a non-refundable deposit and then she won't have a choice. She'll be mad, but hopefully she'll get over it," Lark said. "At least, that's Sydney's idea. I'm not sure if I agree with it."

"Yeah, that sounds like a bad way to book your wedding venue," I said. "Not that I'd know anything about that." I'd never even been to a wedding. The only experience I had with them were movies and other people talking about them. I had no idea if a wedding was in my future or not, but I knew that I wouldn't be spending thousands of dollars I didn't have on it, that was for sure.

"It'll work out. They always work their shit out," Lark said with a smile as she licked her fingers. I handed her a tissue from the box on my coffee table for the rest.

"Thanks," she said. "So, what is the deal with you and Tenley anyway?"

That was an abrupt and unpleasant topic change.

"You know what my deal with her is," I said. "She was that popular girl in high school, and I wasn't. We have been natural enemies ever since."

"So why did you agree to be her fake girlfriend, if you hate her so much?" she asked. Wasn't that the most-important question?

"I'm not going to be her fake girlfriend," I said.

"What did she say when you told her?" she asked, and I couldn't make eye contact with her. "Mia."

"Uh huh," I said, staring into the container of brownies. I definitely needed another one thanks to this conversation.

"You haven't told her," she said, and it wasn't a question.

"I just got home!" I said.

"Do you want to be her fake girlfriend?" Lark asked.

"No! I don't!" I said and Lark pursed her lips as if she didn't believe me.

"It kind of feels like you do," Lark said, shrugging one shoulder.

"I don't, I promise you," I said.

"It's okay if you do. I mean, it's totally weird, but I support your choices, even the weird ones," she said, patting me on the arm. "She is hot, you know."

Of course she was hot. Her level of hotness had nothing to do with it. It was everything else about her that I couldn't stand.

"Fake dating could be fun," Lark said. "All of the fun and none of the complications."

"Lark. She thinks I'm straight," I said.

"So? You're not going to develop feelings for her, right?" she said.

"Absolutely not," I said, making a face. "She's literally the last woman on earth that I would ever fall for."

"Then go for it. See what it's like hanging out with the

people who snubbed you in high school. It's almost like a do-over. Hang out with the popular girl and see if the grass is greener."

I hadn't considered that. While a lot of people had moved on from high school friends, myself included, Tenley had obviously not. If I went to her social media right now, it would be like traveling back in time. All the same people hanging out in all the same places, just with legal alcohol now. It all sounded boring as fuck, but I had to admit, I was curious. I couldn't help it.

I let out a breath.

"I'm only going to go to one party. I only need like, an hour, tops, to see the other side. Then I'm out. An hour is probably as long as I can stand to pretend to like Tenley anyway," I said with a laugh.

"You have to go and then give me constant updates. I'm invested in this," Lark said.

"I will," I said, picking up my phone. "Okay, what the hell do I say to her?"

Lark helped me write out a pretty neutral message to Tenley, asking when and where I needed to show up to be her girlfriend.

There's a party Saturday night at Tommy's. We can start there she sent. **We'll need to go over everything ahead of time so you don't look awkward with me.**

That was a nice little dig that had me fuming.

Who says I'm going to be the awkward one? I responded. **Maybe I'll be an amazing fake girlfriend, you don't even know me.**

I'm not going to half ass this, Mia. I want to get this done so I can get back to my life she sent.

Wow, you're really selling this opportunity to me I responded.

What do you want, money? She sent.

I thought about that for a second. I could really leverage this and make some cash. In addition to being blessed in the looks department, her parents were both doctors and had generational wealth. Truly, she had been handed *everything*.

What was the going rate for a fake girlfriend? I had no idea, and something felt…icky about asking her to pay me.

I didn't want her money.

I'll do it out of the goodness of my heart, how's that I replied.

She typed a response and then deleted it before trying again. **You can just meet me at my house before the party** she sent, along with the address. As if I didn't know where she lived. I mean, I wasn't a stalker or anything, but when you lived in a place like Arrowbridge, you just kind of knew where people lived.

I couldn't lie, I was looking forward to seeing Tenley's house. Sure, it would probably make me hate myself, seeing all the things she could afford, but I'd get a view of the inner sanctum, and you couldn't put a price on that.

The more I thought about this whole situation, the more I realized what I wanted from Tenley wasn't money.

"Well?" Lark asked. I'd forgotten that she was there, I'd been so wrapped up in talking with Tenley.

"She asked if I wanted money, but I'm going to ask her for something else," I said, typing out the message.

I want a favor in exchange for doing this. One big favor from you that I can call in at any time in the future I sent, typing as fast as I could.

I'm not doing anything illegal or embarrassing she responded immediately.

Deal I replied. **We should shake on it in person.**

Fine she sent, and that was the end of the conversation.

"I'm on the edge of my seat here," Lark said, even though

she was sitting deep into my couch. She was working on her second brownie.

"She's going to owe me one huge favor and I'm meeting her at her house on Saturday before a party at Tommy Webb's," I said. Tenley didn't need to tell me where Tommy Webb's house was, because I knew that, too. He'd moved onto his grandparent's farm after they died and spent a lot of time fucking around and occasionally cutting trees and selling weed and having massive parties in the barn that never got the cops called because almost all of them were related to him. He got along with everyone due to hosting the parties and also because he was so stoned out of his mind all the time that it was hard to get mad at him.

"Now I just have to figure out what to wear. No one ever invited me to a barn party in high school so I don't know what the dress code is."

"You want to look good, but not like you made any effort," Lark said, standing up. "Come on."

She led me to my room and started pulling things out of my closet.

"You also need to wear something that you don't mind getting beer spilled on," she said. "But also, you need to look a little slutty if you want to make a man jealous."

"Casual but slutty, got it," I said, trying not to laugh.

"Overalls aren't slutty enough," Lark said, flipping through the hangers in my closet.

"I feel like I should be taking notes or something," I said. "Fashion lessons with Lark."

"I can't help it. I browse fashion social on my breaks," she said. "What about this for bottom?"

She held up a black maxi skirt that had a slit all the way up the leg, so what looked modest at first was actually quite revealing.

"Leg slits are slutty," I said as she tossed it on the bed.

"Boom, wear it with this," she said, adding a short-sleeved dark-green bodysuit that really set off my red hair.

"Wear this with your black boots and some jewelry and you're golden," Lark said, sitting next to me on the bed, careful to avoid the clothes.

"Thanks, friend," I said.

"And wear your hair down," Lark said.

"I will." Most of the time I kept my hair up, but if Lark thought it would look good down, then there was no harm in trying.

"You'll have to send me a pic of the whole fit," she said.

"Don't worry, I will," I said.

"Tenley isn't going to know what hit her," she said.

"I mean, she's not into women, so it doesn't really matter," I said.

"Still, she'll have to pretend she's into you and if you look hot, it'll be easier," she said.

"Do you think she's going to want us to kiss?" I asked.

"Probably," Lark said. "I mean, how else are you going to make her ex jealous? You'll have to get handsy too. Make a real show of it."

I made a face, but a bolt of heat shot through me at the prospect of feeling up Tenley. It wasn't my fault she had a fantastic body that a lot of people would beg to get their hands on. Just because it was fake didn't mean I wasn't going to enjoy it just a little bit.

"It's going to be interesting, that's for sure," I said.

Chapter Three

ON SATURDAY BEFORE THE PARTY, I headed over to Ingrid's to do some work on my toys. I wanted to do a test run with my new mold, and I had a few orders I needed to pack up and get ready to ship. Part of the payment of using her garage was watching Athena while Ingrid took a long shower and had a few minutes of peace not taking care of someone else.

Athena was yelling when I opened the door.

"We're having a rough morning," Ingrid said, and I could see how fried she was in her eyes.

"Go, I've got this," I said, pushing her toward the bathroom. She shuffled off and I went to deal with my screaming niece.

Once I got her calmed down enough to ask her what was wrong, I could see that she was wearing herself out and starting to come back down.

"Do you need a hug?" I asked when she was down to sniffles.

"Yes," she said, her voice thick.

We had a hug and then got her a snack and soon she was back to singing along with her show. I still didn't know what she'd been upset about, but with toddlers you never really knew. They could get upset that their water was wet.

Ingrid came out a while later as I was tidying up. Her hair was wet, but she had on fresh clothes and she seemed much more relaxed.

"Thank you," she said, going over to kiss Athena on the top of her head. "I'm going to make some lunch in a little bit if you want any."

"Sure. I'm just going to work on my orders, so let me know if you need help or anything," I said.

"Will do."

I grabbed the order forms I'd brought with me and passed through the door near the kitchen and into the garage. The shelving unit that Ingrid had helped me build was looking pretty bare. I was going to have to take a whole weekend and do a ton of pouring to catch up. I was also really behind on my custom orders.

What felt like only a few minutes later, Ingrid was calling my name and saying that lunch was ready. I sealed the box I'd been packing and added it to the pile and headed inside to have sandwiches and baby carrots with Ingrid and Athena, then it was back out to do the custom orders.

Customers could not only pick their model, but they could pick the colors of silicone I'd pour together as well as glitter, if they wanted. It had taken a lot of trial and error to learn the right way to pour the silicone with a steady hand so that when it hardened and you took the toy out of the mold, you'd see all the colors and it wouldn't look like a complete disaster. One of the first things I'd invested in was a vacuum pump and chamber to eliminate unsightly air bubbles that would damage the integrity of the toy. I'd mix up the silicone for each toy, add the colors (and glitter, if requested), and then put them in the vacuum chamber to prep all of it to go into the molds.

Pouring could be messy work, which is why I was so

grateful that Ingrid didn't care if I splashed on her garage floor. No matter how careful I was, spills happened. Once I had done as many as I could, I set them all aside to cure, which took hours, so I'd have to come back and pop them out of the molds when they were ready. In the meantime, I had to hope and cross my fingers that I'd done everything right.

I pulled off my gloves and put my mask away and headed back into the house to wash my hands and sit down. Why had I picked two jobs that required so much standing?

"You all done?" Ingrid said, looking up from mopping the kitchen. Athena was down for her afternoon nap, so the house was much quieter.

"For now. Everything is curing," I said, sighing and sitting down. Ingrid finished cleaning and came to join me.

"I'm just hoping you can get your own studio space by the time Athena is in school, so she doesn't nab one of your orders to bring in for show and tell," Ingrid said and we both laughed.

"Don't worry. I'll try to stop that from happening," I said, leaning my head on her shoulder.

"I'm going to a party tonight," I said. My plan had been to not tell Ingrid about Tenley, but I'd also never kept anything from her.

"What party?" Ingrid asked, kicking her feet up on the coffee table.

"Tommy Webb's. One of those barn parties," I said, and Ingrid sat up straight and stared at me.

"We hate those people," she said, incredulous.

"I know. I'm doing a favor for someone," I said, not meeting her eyes.

"Doing a favor for who?" she asked.

I took a breath and braced myself. "Tenley Hill."

"I'm sorry, what did you say?"

"Tenley Hill," I said. "It's a long story, but I'm going with her to the party as a favor and she's going to owe me for it."

Ingrid shook her head at me. "I don't understand most of the words that just came out of your mouth. I thought you hated Tenley?"

"Oh, I do. She makes me miserable every day," I said, nodding.

Ingrid made a frustrated sound. "Does she have something on you? Is it blackmail?"

"No, it's just...look, it's complicated, okay? She came into Common Grounds and she was a mess and I just...offered to help. I can't explain it. But you know I've always wanted to go to one of those parties," I said. Saying that you didn't want to be invited anyway was one way to make yourself feel better about not being invited in the first place.

Ingrid gazed at me for a few seconds and I could see all the thoughts and questions swirling in her mind, but she didn't voice them.

"I think this is a terrible idea, but you already know that it is. I'll just be here to say 'I told you so' when this blows up in your face. And I'll be there to give you a ride if you need, always."

"Wow, so supportive," I said, but I smiled at her.

"Hey, maybe everyone has matured since high school and left petty bullshit behind and you'll have a wonderful time," she said.

"Highly doubtful," I said.

"Mama?" a little voice called from down the hall.

"Duty calls," Ingrid said, getting up.

∽

THAT EVENING before I went over to Tenley's I spent way too long adjusting my outfit and fiddling with my makeup and changing my earrings before I finally forced myself to stop. I took a mirror pic and sent it to Lark, who was out for the day with Sydney.

Hot as fuck she sent in response.

I headed over to Tenley's house and was already annoyed when I parked in her driveway.

The house was new and large and perfect. White, of course, with light blue shutters. If it was owned by someone else, I would have said it was nice, but it was tainted by being owned by Tenley.

I got out and knocked on the door. Loudly, knowing it would annoy her. I was on board with pretending to be her girlfriend, but I was going to make her suffer a little in the process. Otherwise, what was the point? I was going to hold all of this over her for the rest of our lives. Not to mention the favor she owed me. I'd have to come up with something *really* good.

Since Tenley didn't answer the door immediately, I kept knocking, pounding harder and harder until I heard loud cursing on the other side before the door opened.

"Jesus fuck, what is wrong with you?" she said, glaring at me.

"It is I, your fake girlfriend, at your service," I said, doing a little curtsy with the skirt.

Tenley's eyes flicked up and down my outfit, and I saw her take note of the slit in my skirt.

"Well? Do I pass inspection?" I said, executing a little pose, sticking my leg out so it showed.

Tenley rolled her eyes. "Come on."

"Wow, rude," I said, walking into her house. The inside was…completely unexpected. I'd thought everything would be boring and beige and tasteless, but I saw mismatched furniture that looked like she rescued it from a thrift store. There was a mix of vintage pieces with odd colors like mustard and cobalt and emerald and dusty pink with darker woods, but the result wasn't stifling, it felt…cozy.

The floorplan was modern, with an open concept, but each area was defined by clever furniture and art placement.

"Oh," I said, looking into the living room. In addition to a cheery brick fireplace there were books. So many fucking books. Floor to ceiling books. Books on tables. Books in cabinets. Books stacked on the coffee table.

"Do you, um, read a lot?" I asked, gesturing.

Tenley rolled her eyes and crossed her arms. "Obviously."

Ignoring her, I headed for the shelves to see just what she had. You could tell so much about a person by what was on their bookshelves.

I grabbed one book at random and pulled it off the shelf.

"Oh," I said for a different reason when I read the title. It was a writing craft book about erotica.

I held it up so Tenley could see the front of it.

"Give me that," she said, snatching the book away from me and jamming it back on the shelf. "You're not here to judge my books, you're here to practice making my boyfriend jealous."

"Isn't he your ex-boyfriend?" I asked, wanting to yank another book to piss her off.

"If we're going to do this, you're going to have to stop saying shit like that," Tenley said, pointing her finger at me. For the first time since I'd walked in, I took note of her outfit instead of the inside of the house.

She wore stonewashed wide-leg jeans and a cropped logo sweatshirt with gold earrings and her hair in a low bun. Casual, but still like she'd put in some effort. Her chunky off-white sneakers were just a little too clean.

Her lips were glossy and pink, and I stared at them for a beat too long.

"What?" I asked.

Tenley snapped her fingers at me. "Focus. We're going to

have to act like we're together in like an hour and this isn't going to cut it." She gestured at the space between us.

My mouth was suddenly dry, and I wished I had some water or something. I licked my lips instead.

"Okay," I said. "What did you have in mind?"

"We're going to have to be in each other's space," she said, stepping closer to me. "Just, uh, pretend I'm a really hot guy."

I swallowed hard. "Right. A hot guy." Because I was straight. Straighty McStraightlady. No lesbians here, no ma'am.

Realizing we were getting nowhere, I took the initiative and fully entered her space. I'd always been aware that Tenley was a few inches taller than me, but now it was apparent as I looked up into her face.

"Are those lash extensions?" I asked, my voice hitching. It was a crime how pretty she was, even this close. Shit, where was she hiding her pores?

"Yes," she said, audibly swallowing.

"They're good," I said. "I mean, they don't look too aggressive or fake."

"Thank you," she said and then jumped as I put my hand on her waist.

"Sorry. Should have warned you," I said.

"No, it's okay," she said. "We both need to get used to it."

I'd touched a few women's waists in my day, but for some reason being with Tenley made me feel brand new. Fresh from the closet, scared to make eye contact with a gorgeous woman. I hadn't felt this way in a while. I hadn't gone wild in college, but I'd had my fair share of experiences after denying myself for so long.

"So what should I..." she said, trailing off.

"What would you do if I were Shane?" I asked.

She huffed out a breath that brushed against my cheeks.

"Shane is taller than me," she said, her tone frustrated.

"So? Come on, Tenley, this was your idea," I said. "Suck it up and touch me." She was being way too dramatic about this.

She rolled her eyes, which seemed to be a perpetual habit, and finally lifted her arms to my shoulders, sliding them around me as if we were slow dancing. It was a start.

Tenley inhaled through her nose and I put my other hand on her waist, exerting just a little force to pull her closer until our bodies were almost completely pressed up against each other.

"There," I said. "This isn't the worst thing in the world to happen to you, is it?"

She looked down into my eyes and I tried again not to be jealous of her lash extensions.

"Are you okay?" I asked. She trembled ever so slightly against me.

"Yeah," she said, blinking dazedly.

"Okay," I said. "The holding is fine, but we should probably try something else." Not that I was complaining. Holding onto Tenley wasn't completely horrible. I'd kept my hands on her jeans so I wasn't touching that little strip of skin between her pants and her crop top. That seemed a little too much for this first little experiment.

"What else should we try?" she said. Why was I having to take the lead here?

"I don't know, probably a kiss," I said. "It would be weird if we're completely obsessed with each other if we didn't kiss at least once." My argument was pure logic.

Tenley licked her lips. "I've never kissed a woman before."

"Not even when you were drunk or on a dare?" I asked. Kissing a woman for her boyfriend's amusement and arousal seemed like something she would have done before.

"No," she said, and her fingers fluttered on my back. She was nervous and twitchy.

"It's not that big a deal," I said. "People kiss other people they're not attracted to all the time. Come on, suck it up."

She made a face. "I will not be doing any sucking."

"Fucking hell, Tenley, just kiss me."

When she didn't, I took matters into my own hands, sliding one hand from her waist to the back of her neck and angling her head down before pressing my lips to hers. A simple, casual kiss. A moment. A second. A breath.

"There," I said, my eyes opening. "No big deal, right?"

I waited for her to say something, but then her mouth pressed against mine and suddenly, I was no longer in control. I'd kept my lips closed and the contact light on purpose, but that wasn't what was happening with this second kiss. This wasn't light or soft.

Tenley's kiss was strong and relentless. Tongues were involved. I couldn't breathe and it wasn't important.

Tenley must *really* love her boyfriend if this was the way she kissed him.

I kept hearing strange sounds and realized they were moans and they weren't only coming from me. She was gasping and gripping at me as if she wanted more of me.

All at once, I ripped myself away from her, stumbling against a table with a pile of books on it.

"Yeah, I'd say you've got the hang of it," I said, putting my hand to my chest to make sure my heart wasn't trying to bust through my ribs. I'd knocked over some of her books, but I couldn't figure out how to pick them up. I was too busy staring at Tenley. She had her hand to her lips, as if making sure they were still attached to her face. She hadn't said anything in a long time.

"Tenley?" I asked. She blinked once and gave herself a little shake.

"I think that's enough practice," she said, her voice sharp.

I thought about pointing out that she had been the one to kiss me like that, but I kept my mouth shut.

Better to just let it go.

∼

THE REALITY of the barn party turned out to match up almost exactly with what I'd thought it would be like. Lots of cheap beer, a fire pit outside, a rickety beer pong table, and music so loud that it punched at your eardrums.

Tenley had driven us, and she had clamped onto my hand when we'd gotten out of the car.

"Remember to be into me. Obsessed with me. We have to make it real," she said, squeezing my hand. There was desperation in her voice, and I wanted to stop and ask her if she really wanted to do this. If Shane was worth all this trouble. Because from where I was standing, he was a shitty human and she was definitely better off without him. She was the prettiest girl in Arrowbridge, and she could have any guy she wanted. Why waste it on some dude who peaked in high school? It made no sense.

Once again, I kept my mouth shut and followed her into the party. The barn doors were wide open, and I recognized just about everyone here. For a moment I had the feeling of time collapsing in on itself. These people would probably be here in ten years, twenty years. Getting drunk in this barn and telling the same stories. How tiring.

"Should we get a drink?" I asked Tenley as just about everyone stared at her as we walked in together. I couldn't tell if they were staring because of the thing that happened with Shane, or because of me, or both.

It was probably both.

"Yes," Tenley said, smiling at me and yanking me close to her before kissing me. Everything in the barn faded, even the sound, and the only thing that existed was Tenley's mouth on mine. Her fingers digging into my hand. Her other hand tenderly pressed against my cheek.

My hands had gone to her waist again, and this time I hadn't avoided touching her skin directly. She was warm and so soft. How long had it been since I'd made out with anyone? A while. Way too long.

At some point a new sound penetrated my consciousness. Cheers and hoots and hollers.

Tenley made a little frustrated sound in her throat and then pulled back. I kept my eyes closed. I didn't want to open them and see everyone staring at us.

"Let's get a drink," Tenley said, tugging me even though I stumbled. I had no option but to open my eyes and find that most everyone was staring at us, including Shane, who had his arm slung around a woman who had bullied me in high school. Shane's face was murderous. Her face was pure disgust.

"Tenley, what the hell?"

A few people had flocked toward us as Tenley shoved a can of cheap beer into my hand. I cracked the top and sipped, cringing. It was cold, but that was about it. I much preferred a mixed drink, or even wine from a box. Still, Tenley was driving, so I might as well take advantage and get buzzed.

Tenley had let go of my hand, but I stood close to her as her friends bombarded her with questions about, well, me.

"It just kind of happened, but I'm soooo happy. Right, babe?" Tenley said, leaning into me.

I guess we were doing cutesy nicknames. Hadn't discussed that ahead of time, but we'd both been way too distracted by the kissing to discuss that part. We were winging it now.

"Literally so happy, babe," I said, making my voice super sweet. Tenley stepped on my foot just enough to hurt.

"Awww, that's so sweet. We completely support you," one of the women said and the other two nodded.

"One of my cousins is a lesbian," one of them said.

"Yes, love is love!"

I had to fight not to make gagging noises, but I kept a smile plastered on my face and drank the rest of the beer faster than I normally would have just so I didn't have to say anything else.

"Yeah, thanks," Tenley said, but I could tell her attention was on Shane and his new woman, Cassie. They also seemed pretty wrapped around each other. Cassie had that "adoring gaze" thing going on and was laughing way too hard at everything he said. Gross.

Unsure of what to do, I just let myself be led around by Tenley as I tried not to die of boredom. I hated just about everyone here. Why had I thought this would be anything but awful? I hadn't needed to come to this party to know what it was going to be like and now here I was and all I wanted was to leave and never see any of these people ever again.

"Where's the bathroom?" I finally asked Tenley, my voice a little too loud. She had us camped out in a corner of the party as she glared at Shane and would mutter things to herself every now and then.

"Oh, it's in the house," she said, pointing. A lot of the guys hadn't even bothered with the toilet and just relieved themselves outside into a bush, but there was no fucking way I was doing that.

"Why don't you come with me, BABE," I said, putting emphasis on the last word.

Tenley blinked at me. "Oh, of course."

Reluctantly, we headed out a side door and across a small patch of dead lawn to the house. I bet Tommy's grandparents wouldn't be too pleased to see how much he'd absolutely trashed their property, but it wasn't my business. The house had a distinct odor that I couldn't put my finger on, but I didn't want to be in here any longer than I had to.

"This way," Tenley said. She'd dropped my hand the

second we'd come into the house, and it was as if she'd slid a sheet of ice between us. No longer was she pulling me closer and sharing warm smiles. No, she was back to the woman who annoyed me every damn day in the coffee shop and demanded free drinks.

I didn't really have to pee, but I figured I might as well go while I was here, so I went into the bathroom and did my thing before coming out and finding Tenley doing something with her phone.

"Your turn," I said, gesturing.

"I'm fine," she said, not looking up.

"Tenley," I said, and she finally met my eyes. "What the hell are we doing here?"

She gave me a look as if I'd said something ridiculous. "We're here to make Shane jealous. Like you agreed to. Remember?" She made sure to emphasize the last word, like she was speaking to a child.

"Yes, I'm aware. Believe me, I'm aware. But you seem…" I trailed off.

"What, Mia? I seem what?" Her voice was sharp enough to cut glass.

"Shane is an asshole! He's always been an asshole. I think you've been with him so long you don't see it, or love is blind or whatever, but holy shit, Tenley, Shane is the absolute worst," I said.

"You don't even know him!" We were truly yelling at each other now, but this confrontation was kind of inevitable.

"I think I remember high school. The time he stole that kid's wheelchair? Setting the chemistry lab on fire? Streaking through the assembly about dating violence? And that's not even touching on all the racist, homophobic, bigoted, and other shitty comments he's made," I said.

Tenley crossed her arms and glared daggers at me, her face bright red.

"You don't know him," she said.

"I think I know him just fine. I think you're the one who doesn't see him, but that's on you. I'm over it," I said, and headed for the front door.

It didn't matter what she offered me; I was not doing this anymore. I reached her car and realized that I didn't have a way home. Tenley had driven us.

"I'm assuming you don't know how to hot-wire a car," a voice said behind me.

"No, but I can probably Google it," I said, turning around to find Tenley standing behind me. Huh. She'd followed me.

She leaned against the car and sighed. "Shane is…he's complicated, okay? When I say you don't know him, I mean it. He's had a lot of crap go wrong in his life. I know he's not perfect, but the person he is when we're together? I love him, and I don't know what I'd do without him. We've been together for so long because we love each other. He loves me. I know he does."

To anyone, it would be obvious that Tenley was so deep in denial, she was buying real estate and putting down roots. It was sad, honestly. How awful to be in love with someone so terrible.

"Every year on my birthday, he takes me to a different theme park. He wakes me up and tells me to get in the car and we drive. I never know where we're going to end up. We went to Disney World once and he had matching ears for us in the trunk the whole time. He rented a beautiful hotel in the park and went on any ride I wanted to," Tenley said. "He brings my mother flowers randomly. He volunteers at the animal shelter on the weekends walking the dogs."

She was really trying to convince me. It wasn't that I didn't believe he did those things. Guys like Shane almost always treated the people they valued well. It was how they treated everyone else that was the problem. It didn't matter if you saved puppies if you made racist comments about the server at a restaurant an hour later. Tenley knew this. She had to.

Tears started to drip down her face and my anger at her evaporated. Now she just looked pathetic.

"I love him," she said, shrugging. "He was there in my life and then he was gone and there's this huge fucking hole and everything is different, and I hate it. I hate my life."

She stomped her foot and looked away from me, tears still falling. I crumbled and pulled her into a hug.

"Hey, it's okay," I said, rubbing her back as she cried on my shoulder. "It's going to be okay."

Tenley started to sob and I kind of wished one of her friends were here instead of me, but that wasn't what had happened.

"Shhh, it's okay," I said, trying to be as comforting as I could while I could literally feel my shirt getting wet.

At last Tenley sniffed and stood up, wiping her eyes. She still looked gorgeous, but that was beside the point.

"Come on," I said, dragging her back into the bathroom. I pushed her against the sink and grabbed some toilet paper when I couldn't find tissues.

"Here," I said, dabbing at her face with the paper. I'd thought she was going to snatch it out of my hand and do it herself, but she didn't. Once I had her face cleaned up, I gave her some more so she could blow her nose. She checked herself out in the mirror and groaned.

"I look trashed," she said.

"You don't, I promise," I said. Tenley wet some more paper and swiped at her face again before taking a few deep breaths.

"You good?" I asked.

She nodded. "Yeah, I'm good." She reached into her bag and pulled out a lip balm and applied it with a steady hand in the mirror. Tenley pouted once and then swept out of the bathroom.

"Okay," I said. She turned around and held out her hand. "Coming?"

∼

AN HOUR later I was decidedly tipsy and having a much better time. I wasn't having a *good* time, but better.

"You are such a lightweight," Tenley said as I leaned against her and did a little dance.

"You know me, BABE," I said, emphasizing the word again and then laughing.

"Hey, Tens," a voice said, and Tenley's spine snapped straight.

"Hey, Shane," she said, her voice soft and breathy.

"So I see you've, uh, moved on," he said, refusing to look at me.

"Clearly I have," she said, yanking me closer and pulling me off-balance so I fell into her.

Shane looked at me and then laughed before leaning in to say something in Tenley's ear. Her eyes went wide and then Shane winked at her and sauntered off.

"What did he say?" I asked her as she watched him go.

"Nothing," she said, shaking her head. "Let's go."

She yanked me out to the car, and it was a miracle I didn't trip all over my feet in the dark. The ground also wasn't that even.

"What did he say?" I asked as I clutched the car door. Tenley unlocked the car and got in. I managed to slump into my seat and get my seatbelt on.

"You okay?" I asked as Tenley maneuvered the car around the others and back onto the main road.

"I'm fine," she said, her teeth clenched.

"Okie dokie," I said, giving her a thumbs up.

Tenley didn't say a word until we arrived back at her house.

"I probably shouldn't drive right now," I said.

"Fine, whatever. You can come in and wait it out," she said, and I followed her into the house. "Do you want some water or something?" she asked.

"Yeah, that would be great," I said, venturing back into her living room and eyeing the books.

"How about tea?" Tenley called from the kitchen.

"Perfect," I called back as I sat myself down on the dusty pink sofa. This was the kind of couch you could drape yourself on while wearing a fabulous gown.

Tenley came into the room carrying a tray with not only tea, but mini croissants, two types of jam, and butter along with honey, lemon, and sugar for the tea.

"Wow," I said as she set it down on the coffee table.

"I figured you might want a snack," she said, taking a seat beside me.

"Thank you," I said, genuinely surprised. This was quite the spread.

I made up a cup of tea and spread butter and blackberry jam on one of the croissants.

"This is the fanciest drunk food I've ever had," I said, shoving almost the entire croissant into my mouth in one go.

"It's not that fancy," Tenley said, stirring her tea and then sipping.

"Still," I said. "I didn't expect tea and croissants."

"What did you expect?" she asked, turning to look at me.

"I…" I said, trailing off. "I don't even know. I guess I didn't really picture actually hanging out with you. Not like this anyway." Definitely not sitting and sipping tea on her vintage couch after a party.

"There's more to me than meets the eye, Mia," she said, carefully slicing a croissant in half.

"I'm beginning to see that," I said.

Tenley buttered her croissant and added a layer of jam

before taking a dainty bite. Something about the way she did it made me laugh.

"What?" she said, her hand going to her face.

"Nothing," I said, looking away. "Are we going to talk about your massive book collection or no?"

Tenley shrugged. "We can, if you want."

"Are they decorative, or have you actually read them?" I asked.

"That's a patronizing question," Tenley said, bristling. "Does it matter?"

I shrugged. "I guess not. But if you'd read a lot of them, then I'd ask which ones were your favorite and if I could borrow one." Some people were too precious about books, in my opinion. If someone wanted to have rainbow bookshelves of books they'd never read, it didn't really affect me. I mean, I didn't even own a ton of physical books since my apartment was small and they were a bitch to move. But I had endless ebooks on my phone, and that was fucking great.

"Yes, Mia, I've read them. Well, almost all of them. My TBR is around," she said, gesturing.

"I'm assuming you've been to Mainely Books then," I said, and Tenley glared at me.

"Yes. Kendra and I are on good terms," she said.

"You're not in the book club, though?" I asked. "I mean, I know the books we mostly read are sapphic romance so maybe you're not into that."

Just a quick glance of the book spines showed me more than a few sapphic romances that I recognized, which was interesting. She also had a ton of other books, so I couldn't say anything for sure, but I still made note of it. Not that you had to be sapphic to read those books, but it made more sense on why she'd be fine with fake dating me, and not choosing a guy instead. I mean, fake coming out to your whole social circle was kind of a big deal for someone like Tenley. They weren't the most progressive bunch, which was one of the main reasons I never wanted to hang out with them. Tonight had been more than enough.

"I'm not really a book club person," she said, selecting another croissant.

"You should try it," I said, and then wanted to reel those words back in. I didn't need to invite Tenley into another part of my life. I saw her at work enough as it was.

"Maybe," she said, but her voice wasn't enthusiastic, which was a relief.

"Since we're sitting here, recommend a book to me," I said. If she owned this many books, she must want to show off a little. Brag on her collection.

"That's not something I can just do without knowing your tastes," she said.

"Okay, fine. How about a really steamy romantasy?" I asked. I hadn't specified sapphic, so I wanted to see what she'd grab.

Tenley thought for a few seconds before getting up and pulling several books off her shelves and then setting them in my lap. One was a bestseller that I'd read years ago, so I set that aside, and then read the back of a second, but it didn't call to me. The third, though, that one was sapphic and pushed all my buttons.

"What happens to me if I don't return it?" I asked. Not that I planned on doing that. I respected people's books.

"Then I hunt you down and kill you slowly via papercuts all over your body," Tenley said, her eyes narrowed to slits.

"Okay, noted. I will take good care of it," I said, holding the book to my chest.

"No dog-earing the pages, no food as bookmarks, no using it as a coaster, no coffee or liquids anywhere near it, you got it?" Tenley said, pointing at me.

"I've got it, Tenley, I promise I'll treat it like one of my own," I said.

Tenley let out a breath. "Good."

I wanted to ask her why she'd picked a sapphic romance for me, seeing as how I was a straight lady, but I didn't want to draw attention to myself like that and then have to lie again, so I didn't.

I set the book aside and went back to the first book she'd given me.

"Have you read this one?" I asked.

~

IT TURNED out the way to get Tenley talking was to ask her about books, holy shit. It was like turning on a fire hose. Once she started, she didn't stop. Normally I might have been annoyed at someone completely monopolizing a conversation like that, but she was so animated and so excited that she kept stumbling over her words and barely taking a breath. She'd been modest when she said she'd read most of the books she had, because holy shit had she read a lot of books. It made me feel like a bad reader in comparison. As soon as I was completely sober, I was overhauling my TBR and getting my ass in gear. Sometimes work was draining, and I didn't have the energy to read when I got home, but that was going to change. I couldn't let my fake girlfriend read more books than me.

It wasn't until I started nodding off that I realized how fucking late it was. We'd been sitting here for hours.

"Uh I should get home," I said.

"Oh, yeah," Tenley said, nodding, her face getting a little red.

"Thank you," I said, reaching out and putting my hand on hers. "Thank you for the tea and everything. And the book."

"Sure," she said, and I stood up. I was definitely sober

enough to get myself home, but a small part of me wanted to pretend I was still wasted, and that thought really shook me so much that I knew it was definitely time to go. Spending too much time with Tenley was warping my brain.

"So, uh, I guess I'll see you on Monday at the coffee shop," I said as she walked me to the door.

Tenley nodded. "You will. I like my routine."

I could tell. She seemed better than she'd been that day when she'd come in like a mess. Tonight probably hadn't gone the way she intended, but it hadn't been all bad, I didn't think.

"Drive safe, Mia," she said, leaning in the doorway. There was absolutely no reason for us to kiss now, with no one watching, but leaving without a kiss made me feel like the night was…unfinished.

"I will," I said to her and a tendril of hair fell against her cheek. The urge to tuck it behind her ear was so intense, I had to clench the hand that wasn't holding onto the book she'd let me borrow.

Tenley inhaled once and then backed one step into the house. I managed to get a hold of myself and turn around to head to my car.

Chapter Four

"How's your fake girlfriend?" Lark asked when I came over for brunch on Sunday. It was something she did every now and then and I had to admit, I was a big fan. Today she was making some sort of breakfast casserole with tortillas and black beans and salsa and other veggies and eggs on top. I was using her new milk frother to make myself a latte and Sydney was sorting through her massive hot sauce collection, trying to decide which one to drench her breakfast with.

"You know what happened. I was literally messaging you the whole time," I said. At least I had been when I'd been more sober. When I was buzzed the messages had gotten a little sparse and then there was that whole other situation with Tenley that I'd decided I wasn't going to tell her about. Not to mention the time I'd spent at Tenley's. And the book she'd lent me. I hadn't started it yet, but that was what I was going to spend my afternoon doing. No, I wasn't going to be telling Lark about any of that.

I yawned as Lark shoved the casserole in the oven and set the timer.

"I feel like there's something you're not telling me," she said, crossing her arms.

"I didn't tell you every single detail, but you got the main points," I said, finishing my latte. I definitely needed another one to get me through this day. I definitely hadn't slept enough to be awake right now. Maybe before I settled in to read, I'd take a nap.

"Uh huh," Lark said, but she didn't seem convinced.

"Tommy's house was disgusting, did I tell you that?" I said, trying to steer the topic in another direction.

"I'm not surprised at all," Sydney said from her position on the couch. She was reading our book club pick for this month, the first in a contemporary series that centered around a coffee shop owned by married lesbians. I hadn't started it yet, but I was looking forward to it, especially considering that it had a protagonist in her 40s, so there was an age gap between her and her love interest. Age gaps were one of my auto-read tropes. Along with rivals to lovers. I liked the drama.

"Tommy was that kid who went to the bathroom and when he came back you know he didn't wash his hands," Sydney said, peeking over the back of the couch and making a face.

I shuddered and realized that I should have brought up something else.

"What's Tenley's house like?" Lark asked, pouring some coffee for herself.

"Oh, it's nice," I said, going to the fridge for more milk to make another latte.

"And?" Lark said. "Details."

I should have just taken a few covert pictures and sent them to her. Ingrid had also sent me a ton of questions via text, and I'd kept things vague for her too.

"It's decorated really nice. She's got some pretty vintage furniture. I thought she'd be into more modern stuff, but there was nothing from IKEA in there," I said. Not even the bookshelves. They were mismatched but worked together. Tenley had a beautiful eye for decorating and seeing how things that you wouldn't think would go together did.

"Huh," Lark said. "Looking at her I would have thought she'd be into boring and beige. No color. No flavor."

"I know," I said, pouring milk into the frother. "It was a surprise."

"People can surprise you," Lark said.

"Yeah," I said, not looking at her.

Lark must have sensed my reluctance to talk further about the night before, so she moved on to other things that didn't involve Tenley. That didn't mean I wasn't thinking about Tenley. Wondering what she did on the weekends. Would she pick a book from those shelves and drape herself on the mustard velvet couch with a cup of tea steaming beside her as the soft afternoon light filtered through the curtains? Why was I picturing this in such great detail?

"Mia?" Lark said.

"Huh?" I asked her.

"I asked you if you've started the book club book," Mia said. We'd finished our brunch and were now just hanging out as Sydney read in the library guest room. Sydney was great, but it was also really fun to have time for just me and Lark. If I'd been paying attention to her and not writing fanfiction about Tenley in my mind.

"Oh, no. I have a different book I have to finish first," I said. The book Tenley had given me, that I couldn't wait to start.

"Need more coffee?" she asked when I yawned again.

"No, probably just a nap," I said, covering my mouth as my jaw cracked with another yawn. "Having to smile in front of terrible people from high school was exhausting."

"I bet," she said. "You couldn't pay me to spend even five minutes with the mean girls from high school." Lark had gone to some super fancy private school, and it sounded like a hellish experience. The stories she told me sometimes sounded like they came from some TV drama.

"Still haven't told her you're a giant lesbian have you?" Lark said.

"No, and I'm not going to, if I can help it. I don't want to make things weird," I said.

"Oh, I'd say it's already pretty weird," Lark said, snorting. "Wouldn't be me pretending to be heterosexual for a girl from high school."

"It's not like that," I said, but it was exactly like that.

"It'll be a funny story you can tell down the road, I suppose," she said.

"Yeah, definitely," I said, yawning again. Lark pulled me to my feet and shoved me down the hall to my apartment with orders for a nap. I fell onto the couch and completely passed out until I woke up at 6 p.m. wondering what the hell happened.

So much for my afternoon of reading.

∽

"THERE'S YOUR FAKE GIRLFRIEND," Lark said, bumping against me to get my attention on Monday morning.

I looked up to see a fresh-looking Tenley setting her bag down at her usual table before sauntering over to get in line. She made eye contact with me and gave me a little wave. I nodded back at her and went back to what I was doing. What was I doing again? Right. Latte. I was making a three-shot latte.

Lark practically shoved me toward the register when it was Tenley's turn to order. She had another crop top on today, this one was short sleeved, and she'd paired it with ripped-to-hell jeans that were more holes than fabric.

"Good morning," she said, leaning over the counter and tilting her chin forward. I stared at her for a second. Was she expecting me to kiss her? We hadn't discussed what we were doing outside of parties at all.

"Um," I said, unable to stop staring at her puckered mouth.

"No kiss for me?" she said.

"Not while I'm working," I said, and she pulled back.

"Fine," she said, but I didn't miss the flash of disappointment on her face. She was really laying it on thick. "I'll have that fruity strawberry thing. Iced. Large. And a chocolate croissant."

I tapped in the order and she paid, winking at me before sliding over to the pickup area.

"What the fuck was that?" Lark said in my ear, low enough so no one else could ear.

"I don't know," I hissed back before I smiled at the next customer, one of my regulars who was an older guy who worked for the postal service.

Since Tenley had messed with me earlier, I went ahead and decided to mess with her a little bit back.

"Sevenly? Sevenly?" I called out when I finished her drink and set her croissant on a plate.

Tenley was right there, glaring at me.

"Cute," she said, snatching the drink and the plate.

"I'm not the one named after a number," I said.

"You're *hilarious*," she said as she grabbed some napkins and headed to her table, but I couldn't help smiling.

～

I'D HALF-EXPECTED her to come over and bug me again, but she did her normal thing of getting out her computer and typing away, staring at the screen in concentration and occasionally muttering to herself, pink headphones firmly on her ears.

It wasn't until my break that she spoke to me again. I was on the picnic table, shoving a bagel in my face and scrolling through social when someone sat next to me.

"Watcha looking at?" she said, scaring me so much that I almost dropped my bagel.

"Holy shit, you scared me," I said, putting my bagel down. "Can you read the sign?" I pointed to the EMPLOYEES ONLY sign on the wall.

"Yes, I can read it, but I'm choosing to ignore it," she said, leaning back and tilting her face upward.

"What the hell was that kiss thing earlier? Kissing outside of parties wasn't part of our deal," I said, doing my best not to watch how her hair lit up in the sun, and how pink her lips were.

Tenley laughed and looked at me. "Oh, I know. I just wanted to see your reaction. Totally worth it."

I scowled at her and she giggled, and the sound was so adorable that I could barely stand it. This giggle was a very different sound than the laugh she'd used with her friends last night. Or maybe I was just imagining things.

"You're lucky I don't spit in your macchiatos," I said, even though it was something I'd never do.

"You wouldn't," Tenley said, taking her hair down so it tumbled over her shoulders and then combing her fingers through it. "You're too much of a rule follower."

I scoffed. "I'm not a rule follower."

"Please, high school was not that long ago," she said, twisting her hair up again.

"You didn't notice me in high school," I said, snorting. None of those people noticed me, unless it was to make some sort of mean comment. Tenley had never been someone who'd done that, but she'd stood there and said nothing.

"I noticed you in high school. You were just too cool for the rest of us," she said, and I blinked at her.

"What the fuck are you talking about?"

She studied her nails, picking at one of them.

"Oh, you know. You weren't into the same stuff as the rest of us," she said.

I had no idea what she was even saying.

"Yes I was," I said.

"You didn't act like it," she said, glancing over at me. My break was almost over, but I was completely distracted by Tenley.

"What did I act like?" I asked.

"Kinda snobby, actually. Like you had better things to do than go to dances and hang out and try to sneak off-campus for lunch," she said.

"I'm not a snob!" I said, sitting up straight.

"I didn't say you were! I said you acted like you were. Shit, Mia, that was a long time ago. Let it go. You probably thought I was a bitch in high school," she said.

"I did."

She smiled. "Well, at least that was true. I am a bitch."

The timer on my phone signaling the end of my break went off and I looked down at my half-eaten bagel.

My break was almost over, so I shoved as much bagel into my mouth as I could fit without choking.

"You might want to chew that," Tenley said.

"Thanks," I said, but it came out muffled.

"See you back in there," Tenley said, walking around the building to go back in the front door since she couldn't just waltz in the employee entrance. At least she respected that rule.

Somehow, I managed to get my bagel down without dying and wiped my face quickly before heading back behind the counter to relieve Lark so she could go on her break.

"When I get back, details," she said pointing as she headed past me.

∽

WHEN LARK RETURNED from her break, we were fully in the mid-morning lull, so there was no way to really avoid talking about the Tenley situation.

All of my energy was currently on not noticing Tenley, while simultaneously noticing every fucking thing about her. Her table was right in a ray of sunlight that lit her up like some sort of angel.

"I don't know what her deal is. Every time I try to talk to her, I feel like I get all turned around and we end up talking about something else," I said. "She's so…infuriating." I kept my voice low, even though Tenley had headphones on and wasn't listening to me.

"Hot and infuriating, which is a sexy combination," Lark said, singing the last two words. Recently she'd started going to local open mic nights and sharing her talent. When we'd first become friends, I'd had no idea she had a beautiful voice and then I wouldn't stop telling her that she should be singing in public, or at the very least recording her stuff. Sydney agreed with me, so we'd basically bullied her into giving it a shot. I always told her to remember me when she got famous.

"She's not sexy," I said, clenching my teeth.

"We both know that's a lie," Lark said, laughing under her breath. "Too bad she's straight."

"*Such* a tragedy," I said, letting the sarcasm drip.

∽

TENLEY STAYED until the end of my shift and when I headed out to my car, she was standing nearby.

"I think this officially qualifies as stalking," I said.

"It's not stalking if we ended up leaving at the same time," she said, unlocking her car and tossing her bag onto the passenger seat.

"Fine. I'm going to go home now," I said, doing the same with my bag. My feet were angry and all I wanted to do was sit down and not have to smile for a few hours. None of that involved chatting with Tenley. I'd also probably wander over to Lark and Sydney's and steal some of their food.

Tenley had a look on her face like she wanted to say something else, but then she nodded and opened her car door.

"See you tomorrow, Mia," she said before shutting her door and turning on music so loud I could feel the bass thumping through my chest.

I shook my head at her and got into my vehicle and headed back to my apartment.

～

THAT NIGHT I finally got to start the book Tenley had loaned me. I made sure I'd scrubbed my hands really well before I even picked it up. I didn't want to ruin it. I also had a beautiful wooden bookmark that my sister had gotten me for my last birthday. No receipts or crap like that. I also made sure I'd cleaned off my coffee table so it wouldn't get stained when I set it down. That was probably overkill, but I wanted to be safe.

I was just turning to the first chapter when my phone went off with a call from my sister.

"Hey, I feel like we haven't talked in forever," she said, and I could hear Athena in the background singing along to one of her shows.

"I was literally at your house on Saturday," I said.

"I know, but it still feels like a long time. Have you seen Tenley since the party?" she asked.

"Yeah, she was in today. It was weird." Ingrid waited for me to say more, but I didn't.

"Weird how?" she asked.

I still hadn't told Ingrid that the favor I was doing for Tenley was pretending to be her girlfriend. It was honestly shocking that someone hadn't asked her about it yet. Arrowbridge was a small place and gossip traveled faster than wildfire.

"I'm going to tell you what the favor was and I'm going to ask you to not freak out about it, okay?" I said.

"Well now I'm both worried and intrigued," she said.

"Her boyfriend broke up with her and she's using me to make him jealous," I said, bracing myself for Ingrid's response.

She was silent for a few seconds. "Using you how?"

"I'm pretending to date her, okay? That's the favor. Go ahead and judge me now," I said, yanking my couch blanket over my legs.

"I have so many questions right now," Ingrid said. "Is Tenley even queer?"

"No. And she thinks that I'm straight too," I said.

"Mia, what the hell?" Ingrid screeched.

"I know! I know. You don't have to lecture me, okay? I know how messed up this situation is," I said, bristling.

"It's just weird, Mia. Why are you doing this for her?" she asked.

"I don't have a good answer for that. I saw a human in distress and now here I am," I said.

Ingrid let out a breath. "You're going to tell her you're a lesbian at some point, right?"

"Yeah, when all this is over," I said.

"I thought you just had to go to one party?"

Now I was the one sighing. "One party didn't work. There's another one this weekend that I'm going to."

"This sounds like a lot of time and work for a favor," Ingrid said, and there was a tone in her voice that I didn't like.

"I don't like her," I said immediately, to head off those questions.

"Mia," she said. "You obviously don't hate her as much as you thought you did."

"My opinions on her haven't changed, Ing. She's still one of the most annoying people I've ever met." If anything, my annoyance at Tenley had only deepened.

"Okay," Ingrid said. She definitely didn't believe me. "I'm stuck on something else, though. If she's completely straight, why didn't she find a guy to make her ex jealous?"

"I was kind of right there, so I think I was in the wrong place at the right time," I said.

"Huh," she said in the same tone of voice Lark had used when we'd talked about this part of the plan.

"She doesn't care what people think of her, which has always been Tenley," I said.

Ingrid snorted. "If you really think that, then I don't even know what to say."

"What do you mean?" This conversation was really going downhill.

"The reason that Tenley has maintained her popular girl status all these years is because she cares way, way too much what other people think and has created herself to be pleasing to others."

I had to sit with that for a second. I didn't think it was true, but it was something to think about. During my high school career, I'd definitely tried to make myself palatable to the popular people, but no matter what I'd done, nothing had worked. Maybe Tenley was just better at doing it than I was.

"I can't believe my sister is pretending to be straight. I didn't come out of the closet first for you to march right back in," she said, but she was laughing.

Ingrid had first come out as bisexual in high school and then later as a lesbian. She set the bar high for being out, and it made things hard when I decided to wait until college to come out. She'd been supportive, but deep down, I knew she'd judged me a little bit for it, even if she wasn't aware that she had.

"I'm staring at pictures of shirtless men right now, oh my god, men are soooooo hot," I said and that made her burst out laughing.

"Don't catch the straight from your fake girlfriend," she said. "That's how they get you."

"The fact that I told her I was straight, and she didn't immediately call bullshit was truly shocking to me," I said.

"Shoulda been gayer," Ingrid said.

"I'll work on it," I said.

∾

ON TUESDAY, Tenley looked very different when she walked into Common Grounds. Before she could even open her mouth to order, I spoke.

"Are you okay?" She didn't look as devastated as the day of the breakup, but her eyes were red, and she looked completely wilted.

"Yeah," she said, her voice rough. She rubbed her eyes as if she hadn't gotten any sleep. "I don't know what I want." Her voice was hollow.

"It's okay. I know what you like," I said, punching in an order.

Tenley nodded and tried to give me a smile. "Thanks."

"Someone's having a rough day," Lark said, shoveling ice into a cup for an iced coffee order.

"Yeah, I bet it has something to do with her ex. I wish she'd get over him. He's not worth all this," I said.

"For real," she said, shaking her head.

I called out Tenley's order and she came over to get it.

"I thought you might need a cupcake," I said when she saw the additional cupcake on the plate with her croissant.

Tenley picked up the plate and gave me a real smile. It was weak, but it was there.

"I did, thank you," she said. "Did you start the book?"

I laughed. "I stayed up way too late and I couldn't stop until I finished. I need the next book immediately."

I had to get back to work, but the pull to sit down and talk books with Tenley was intense.

"Just wait until you read book two. Just wait," she said, backing away from the counter with her order.

I shook some sense back into myself and I headed back to save Lark from the morning rush.

THIS TIME when I took my break, I wasn't surprised when Tenley sat next to me on the picnic table.

"Rough night?" I asked and she presented me with the cupcake.

"I thought we could split it," she said, unsheathing a plastic knife from her pocket.

"I don't have any money, I'm broke," I said, putting both hands up as if she was robbing me.

"Haha, me neither," she said, cutting the cupcake in half and sliding it over to me.

"Thanks," I said, picking it up. The cupcakes at Common Grounds came from Sweet's Sweets and they were so fucking good, I had to force myself not to eat at least three of them a day. It had been a while since I'd indulged, and my first bite was pure heaven.

"Why haven't I been buying these?" Tenley asked after her first bite.

"No idea. We've both been missing out."

Tenley didn't say anything else until after she'd finished her cupcake and wiped her fingers on a napkin she whipped out of her pocket.

"I was up late crying about Shane," she said. "Just missing him. We used to talk all day, every day. He was the person that I wanted to share something funny with, something sad with. I talked to him about everything and now that I don't have him in my life for that, there's this big hole that I can't stop seeing," she said. "In case you were wondering."

"I was," I said. "But I wasn't going to push you to talk about it if you didn't want to."

She lifted one shoulder in a shrug. "It is what it is. He's gone from my life right now. I just keep telling myself this is temporary and soon we'll be back to normal."

My teeth clamped down on my tongue so I didn't stomp on her dreams. It just didn't seem possible that, at this point, Shane was going to open his eyes and realize, OMG, Tenley is his true love all along (cue music), but to point that out to her felt a little too vicious.

She missed him, and as much as I thought he was a giant piece of shit, she loved him and losing him after being together for that many years was going to be rough. It was going to hurt like hell.

"Anyway, enough of that shit," she said. "What are you doing this weekend?"

"Other than hanging out with my sister and maybe Lark, I have to work."

"You work here on the weekends too?" she said, and I realized I'd slipped and mentioned my second job. My second sexy job.

"No, I just have a side hustle," I said, hoping she wouldn't ask a ton of questions.

"Doing what?" she asked.

"I have an online store," I said.

"Selling…" she said, trying to get me to elaborate.

"Jewelry," I said, panicking.

"Oh, nice, what's it called? My mom's birthday is next month, and she loves earrings," Tenley said, getting out her phone.

"You don't have to do that," I said.

"It's not that big a deal," she said, an expectant look on her face.

"I'm, um, not really selling them right now," I said.

"Okayyyyy," Tenley said, drawing out the word. "I'm getting the vibe that you don't want me to find your shop."

I wanted to argue with her, but I didn't.

"I'm incredibly curious why, but you can have your little secret if you want," she said, putting her phone down. I relaxed, grateful that she didn't continue to pry.

"Just so you know, if you do sex work on the side, I'm not going to judge you. If that's what you were worried about," she said a few moments later.

"Oh, thanks," I said, neither admitting or denying that I did sex work. Was making sex toys considered part of the sex work industry? A lot of people might have different opinions on that.

"I have to have dinner with my family this week," she said, pivoting the conversation.

"Is that a good thing or a bad thing?" I asked. In the time we'd spent together, Tenley had rarely mentioned her family.

"It's…an annoying thing. My parents miss Shane, maybe even more than I do. My brothers miss him too." I'd forgotten that Tenley had three brothers. Two older, one younger.

"That sucks," I said. "My parents moved to France and we

only video chat about once a month. They come back every Christmas, but we're not super close," I said. I loved them, there was nothing wrong with our relationship, we just weren't as tight as I was with Ingrid. They had their own lives and so did we and every now and then we talked and caught up. It worked for all parties involved.

"You're close with your sister, though, right?" Tenley said.

"Yeah, we see each other all the time. I lived with her for a while too," I said.

"Two of my brothers are renting a place together too. They call me every time it gets disgusting like I'm going to come over and be their maid," she said, rolling her eyes, but her tone was fond. "They're monsters, but they're family."

We compared our siblings until my break was over and she headed back to her computer and I went back to making lattes.

"You're all happy," Lark said during a lull.

"Hmm?" I said, looking away from Tenley. Her mood seemed more lifted than when she'd walked in today. I didn't think I was completely responsible, but I knew I'd helped.

"You've been smiling since you got back from your break. I think it's time to admit that you like her," Lark said, nodding in Tenley's direction.

"I don't like her," I said.

"You do. A little bit," Lark said.

"Fine, I like her a little bit. But that doesn't mean I *like her*, like her." Tenley was straight and trying to get back with her ex. You couldn't get much more off-limits than that.

"It's okay if you do. Shit happens," she said. "We've all fallen for the wrong person before."

Yes, but I'd already done that in my life. I didn't need to do it again.

"I'm not going to fall for her. There's way too much history standing in the way. And she's going to get her terrible boyfriend back and then she'll go back to bugging me for free coffee."

"Sure," Lark said. "But don't hate yourself if you do develop a crush."

"I'm not developing a crush," I said, trying to keep my voice down. "I'm going to get some more almond milk." I ran to the back room to end the conversation. Like a coward.

∼

"HEY, FAKE GIRLFRIEND," a voice said while I was cleaning dishes in the sink just before heading home. I didn't have to look up to know who spoke.

"Can I help you?" I asked, keeping my voice sweet.

"There's a party at the Castleton beach on Friday night, and Shane is going to be there, so I need you to come with me," she said.

Ugh. I definitely didn't want to do that, but I was the fake girlfriend and that was my job.

"I'll come on a few conditions," I said, going over to the counter. Lark was pretending not to eavesdrop but doing a bad job of it.

"Such as?" Tenley asked, raising one eyebrow.

"First, you drive. Second, I get to say I want to leave, and we have to go, no matter what. Third, you buy me dinner beforehand. Lobster."

Tenley smirked at me and then laughed. "Done. I'll pick you up at six on Friday." She slapped her hand down on the counter and then went back to her chair.

"You should have been making her buy you food before now," Lark said.

"I know, but I've never been a fake girlfriend before. I'm learning as I go," I said.

"It's very entertaining to watch, so thanks for that," Lark said.

I saluted her. "Happy to help."

∼

TENLEY HUNG out with me on my breaks for the rest of the week, and it got harder and harder not to spend all of my time thinking about her. Even when I was doing something else, her laugh would pop into my head, or I'd think of something funny or interesting that I wanted to share with her. Occasionally, we would send each other messages back and forth, but I didn't want to seem like I was bugging her or contacting her too much. Most of the time I typed out and then deleted my messages. A beach party sounded fun, but it wasn't so fun helping your fake girlfriend get back with her ex. At least I had the lobster dinner to look forward to.

Chapter Five

EVEN THOUGH IT was summer at the beach, nights could be chilly, so I dressed in shorts and a t-shirt, but I also had a cozy sweater and a pair of pants I could change into if I needed. I also had an extra blanket that I folded up and could carry with a yoga strap in case of emergency. I hated being cold.

Tenley arrived on time and wearing a gorgeous flowing green kaftan that made her look like she should be posing in Bali while she was on vacation or something.

"Ready for your lobster dinner?" she asked as I threw my stuff in the backseat.

"Hell yeah. I haven't had lobster in a while."

"I figured we could just go to Pine State in Castleton, since it's so close to the beach," she said.

"Works for me," I said, and she backed out of my driveway.

"So how was your day, fake girlfriend?" she asked, turning the music down. She hadn't been at the shop today. I'd looked up about a thousand times and realized she wasn't there, and I wasn't going to analyze any of that. No way.

"My day was fine, how was yours?" I asked. "I still don't

know what the hell you do all day besides typing on a computer."

"Oh, I'm a writer," she said. I sat up straighter.

"That explains all the books," I said.

"Doesn't it?" she said as we passed from Arrowbridge and headed toward the coast and the beach town of Castleton.

"What kind of stuff do you write?" I asked.

"Novels," she said, and didn't elaborate.

"About?"

"Mostly romance," she said, but there was an edge to her voice that I couldn't put my finger on.

"How many books do you have out?" I asked.

"A few," she said.

"I'm sensing this is a touchy topic for you," I said with a laugh. She was being just as forthcoming about her job as I was about my sex-toy side-hustle.

"Not exactly. I've just had people be shitty about it," she said. I wanted to ask if Shane had been supportive, but I also didn't want to talk about him. We were literally going to see him soon. He didn't have to intrude on our night yet.

The Pine State Bar and Grille was packed when Tenley pulled into the lot. I'd hazard a guess that at least half of the cars parked in the lot were from out of state, or people on vacation. Summer in Maine could be jarring. All of a sudden, there were strangers everywhere and you couldn't find a parking spot at the grocery store and the beach was packed. The coffee shop also got a lot more customers, usually people on their way to Castleton or other more coastal places.

We had to wait for a few minutes for a table, so we stood by the entrance to wait.

"Hey, fake girlfriend. Act like my girlfriend," Tenley said in my ear as she slipped her hand into mine and leaned into me.

I turned and found her looking down at me.

"Kiss me," she said softly, and it was like she flipped a

switch in me. I kissed her, and once I started, I didn't want to stop. Her mouth was warm and soft and skilled. Not to mention she got her tongue involved immediately in a way that had my legs turning to liquid and every thought in my brain fading to nothing. Everything in the world narrowed to the two of us.

And then the hostess called out that our table was ready, and Tenley pulled away. I stumbled a little as she led me to our table. It was set just for two, so we sat across from each other, our legs brushing.

The hostess handed us menus, gave us water, and shared the specials.

"Look at that, a lobster dinner for two," Tenley said, scanning the menu. "Is that what you were looking for?"

The meal came with two lobsters, clams, corn, coleslaw, rolls, and lots of drawn butter.

"As long as I can order shrimp instead of the clams," I said, meeting her eyes.

"Not a clam fan?" she asked.

I shuddered in response. No offense meant to those who liked clams and mussels and oysters, but no. Absolutely not.

"More clams for me then," she said, smiling. Our server came over and I recognized her from the last time I'd been here.

Tenley ordered for us, and I got a small glass of the house white wine.

"So," Tenley said when our order was put in.

"What?" I said and she leaned in.

"Just making conversation, Mia," she said, and there was a flirty tone in her voice. Coming here was a good idea if she wanted us to be seen together in front of people who would bring it back to Shane.

"And what did you want to talk about?" I asked, matching her tone and also leaning in. At the same time, I slid my foot up and down her leg. I'd never done anything like that before, but it seemed like the right move.

Tenley giggled. She actually giggled and blushed and I didn't think it was an act. The combination of the blush and the giggle were doing very strange things to me.

The urge to lean over the table and kiss her right then and there was almost completely overwhelming. I'd always known that Tenley was disgustingly pretty, but being pretty and being attractive to me personally were two different things.

I didn't want Tenley to be attractive. It made things way too complicated. Thinking your fake girlfriend was attractive did not figure into the plan. Definitely needed to stop that nonsense right away.

"Sorry," Tenley said, her face getting even redder. "I did have a question for you, though."

I was almost too scared to ask.

"Okayyy," I said, tentatively.

"How exactly do you make those lavender vanilla macchiatos?" she said, and I relaxed. Coffee drinks were easy to talk about. I told her what supplies we used and where to buy them for herself.

"Does this mean you're not going to come to Common Grounds and annoy me every day?" I asked.

"No, I just need to have the stuff so I can make them on the weekends when you're not working," she said. "No offense to the other people you work with, but they don't make them like you."

Now I was the one who was blushing.

"We all make our drinks the same, Tenley," I said, wishing I had a plate of food to stare at instead of her. First the giggling and now the complimenting.

"Well *I* can taste the difference," she said.

"Do you go to the coffee shop on weekends?" I asked. I

hadn't heard of her doing that. At least, none of my coworkers had mentioned it.

"I'm nicer on the weekends," she said.

"Oh, so what you're saying is that you are nice to everyone else but me, is that it?" I said.

"No. I'm mean to Lark too. I'm just meaner to you, specifically," she said.

"Why?" I asked.

Tenley lifted one shoulder. "It's just fun."

With just three words, she'd completely turned off my attraction to her. Thankfully.

I narrowed my eyes.

"Come on. You have fun with it too," she said, nudging my leg under the table.

"I don't," I said.

"Yeah, you do," she said, nudging me again.

∽

OUR LOBSTER DINNER ARRIVED, and I was looking forward to seeing Tenley dismember a lobster and not make a complete mess.

"Cheers," she said, holding up her lobster. I picked mine up and tapped it to hers, water dribbling out of them onto the plate. I moved my lobster to a new plate and went immediately for the shrimp. Tenley ripped open the steaming bag of clams and I watched as she popped them open to get at the meat inside.

"You should see your face right now," she said, laughing as she dunked a clam in a cup of butter. I'd thought she might be a priss and not want to get dirty with this meal, but I was soon proved wrong.

"Eating clams just isn't right," I said, and she snorted.

"Sorry," she said. "My mind went to a different place." It took me a second to realize exactly where her mind had gone.

"Grow up," I said, chucking a shrimp at her.

"Can't. My brain bought real estate in the gutter. I have a lovely little home there," she said, slurping up the clam. Fuck, now my mind had joined hers. Tenley's mouth glistened with the butter and I had to go back to my shrimp. Thinking about Tenley's mouth and what she could do with it was off-limits for the rest of the night.

∽

THIS WAS NOT Tenley's first lobster rodeo as I watched her get every last bit of meat out of hers without even getting anything on her clothes. She didn't even wear a bib. I'd put mine on, even if it looked silly. I'd rather protect my clothes.

"Have you ever read Lexi Starr?" she asked when we inevitably started talking about books.

"No, what kind of stuff does she write?" I asked.

"I was just wondering," she said, digging around in her lobster claw to see if there was anything left.

"She writes sapphic books, so I thought you might have in book club or something," she mumbled.

I hadn't heard the name, but now I was curious. I committed the name to memory and made a note to look it up later.

"I read all kinds of books," I said. "You don't have to be queer to like a queer romance."

"I *know*," she said, her tone defensive. "I'll read pretty much anything. With the exception of books that say they're romances and then kill one of the main characters. What the hell is that?"

I started to respond, but Tenley was off on one of her rants and I went ahead and just let her go. It was fucking cute. I had flipped back over to her being attractive again. Dammit.

She managed to speak and finish her lobster and didn't pause stop to eat her corn. Tenley simply used a knife to scrape the kernels off the cob.

"Less mess," she said as I watched her.

"But less fun," I said, picking up my cob and gnawing on it like you were supposed to.

"If you say so," she said, scooping up corn with her fork.

By the time I was done with my corn, I needed floss and a face wipe, but it didn't matter.

Tenley gave me her coleslaw, but I couldn't finish it.

"I think I'm done," I said, picking up one of the wet wipes that we'd gotten a stack of with our meal. I was going to need way more than one.

"Your chin is covered in butter," Tenley said, carefully wiping her own fingers.

"I like it that way," I said.

"Is this a new skincare trend I'm unaware of?" she asked.

"I mean, probably. They put butter in coffee, so why not on your face?"

Tenley made a face and shook her head. "I will not be putting butter in my macchiatos, thank you."

"People ask us to," I said. "They'll come in and be shocked that we don't serve their special butter coffee whatever. They also get really upset if you suggest that they can bring their own butter to add to our coffee. Don't do that," I said. I'd had several bad experiences, so I'd learned not to make suggestions like that.

"What else do people ask you to do?" she asked, and I told her some of my best barista stories. Lattes for dogs, people who brought in their own raw milk and wanted me to add it to their coffee, and then there were the people who would make wacky orders just to post film them and post a video online. I'd even been asked to be in several videos, for which I had not-so-politely declined.

"Some people just don't have any home training," Tenley said, shaking her head.

"Yeah, look who's talking," I said. "Didn't your mother ever teach you not to harass service workers?"

"Honestly? No. My mom isn't exactly the nicest person," she said, and then I remembered the few times I'd met Tenley's mother. She was one of those people who defined themselves as a "boy mom" and who enjoyed being rude to those she didn't value.

"Sorry about that," I said.

She waved me off. "It's one of the reasons we don't spend that much time together anymore. Plus, she doesn't exactly approve of my career."

"She doesn't think you should be a writer?" I asked.

"Fuck no," Tenley said, laughing. "I thought she was going to have an actual heart attack when I told her."

"What did you go to school for?" I asked. There was so much we didn't know about each other, in spite of growing up in the same town.

"I went for business, but I was allowed to do an English minor. I wanted to major in English and do a minor in graphic design, but they wouldn't pay for school if I did that, so I taught myself graphic design taking online courses."

That was pretty impressive, I had to admit. When I'd wanted to make my own sex toys, I'd watched a ton of videos and read a ton of articles to teach myself how to do it. I'd also reached out to several other creators who had been incredibly generous with their time and my questions.

"That's really cool," I said.

"Thanks. My parents didn't think so. Every week or so my mom sends me a message asking me when I'm going to get a real job," she said.

"Shit, that's awful," I said. I had no idea there was so much animosity between Tenley and her mother. I'd known her life wasn't perfect, but I'd thought it was pretty easy.

"Do you make good money with writing?" I'd heard Alessi talk about how difficult it could be as an independent author without a publisher to do everything, from the writing to making covers and doing all the marketing. It sounded utterly exhausting.

"Some months are better than others, but I make enough to get by," she said, but I could tell she was just being modest. She probably did much better than she was letting on. That house she lived in couldn't have been cheap.

"Do you ever get readers telling you how much they love your books?" I asked.

"My fan mail can get interesting. Most of it's very sweet, but then there are always weirdos," she said.

The server came to check on us and ask if we wanted dessert. We'd already stayed way too long and needed to get to the party, but I wished we could just stay here and have dessert and then go back to her place and she could let me borrow some more books.

This wasn't a real date, so that wasn't going to happen. Tenley wasn't my real girlfriend.

"No, thank you, we'll just take the check," Tenley said, and I had to hold in a sigh.

Tenley and I both hit the bathroom to wash our hands and check to make sure we still looked cute. I did a quick floss and rinsed my mouth to make sure it was free of corn.

"You know you look good," Tenley said when she thought I was taking too long.

"Thanks," I said, looking over at her. She was absolutely staring at my ass. I looked down to make sure there was nothing on it, and then up at her. Tenley's face went red and she made a huffing noise before getting out her phone.

I didn't want to leave until I made sure there wasn't anything on my butt. I even used my phone to check but didn't see anything.

"Let's go," I said finally, and Tenley didn't take my hand as we left the restaurant.

∼

IT WAS strange to see the beach parking lot so empty. Usually when I came on the weekends in the summer you had to fight for a spot and drive around until you found one.

Tenley parked next to a truck and we got out. The breeze was chilly, but not freezing. Still, I slung my blanket over my shoulder with my bag.

"Let's go, fake girlfriend," she said, holding out her hand.

"After you, fake girlfriend," I said.

Tenley and I made our way under the light of the floodlights toward the walkway and then down onto the sand. It wasn't hard to find the group of noisy people all gathered around a driftwood fire with classic rock blasting.

Tenley dragged me over the sand and my heart kept sinking. All the fun we'd had earlier at dinner evaporated and now I had to pretend. I was suddenly so tired I wanted to lay down in the sand and go to sleep.

"Hey," Tenley said when people spotted us and started cheering. They sure as hell weren't cheering for me. I scanned around the fire and found Shane passing out drinks before poking at the fire.

"You're just in time for fireworks," one of Tenley's friends said as she hugged Tenley. I was greeted warmly, which I hadn't expected, and damp can of beer was pushed into my hand. I didn't want to drink it, so I set it down in the sand and hoped no one noticed.

Shane seemed all excited about the fireworks, so he and a

few of the other guys got the box set up. They definitely weren't allowed on the beach, but they weren't letting that stop them.

"Just be ready to run if the cops come," Tenley said in my ear.

"I would rather not be in a situation that would require me to run from the police, Tenley," I said in her ear.

"Calm down, it'll be fine," she whispered back and squeezed my hand before gently kissing my cheek. It was a sweet gesture that made me catch my breath. For a few moments, I watched the firelight flicker on her gorgeous face. She gazed back at me and there was a sharpness but also a softness in her look that made my heart pound.

We both jumped at the first boom of a firework down the beach. It was nothing like one of the big Fourth of July shows, but it was still fun to watch them go off until the box was empty, and the guys were running back to the fire.

"No sirens yet," I muttered to Tenley.

"See? We're fine."

Only a few minutes later, Shane sauntered over. He and Tenley really did make a beautiful couple together. Classic prom queen and quarterback looks. As if nature had created them as part of a matched set.

"Hey, Tens," Shane said in that soft voice. Tenley let go of my hand.

"Hi, Shane," she said, and he blathered on about the fireworks, his words stringing together. I had to admit, it was kind of cute how excited he was about it. Like a little boy with an exploding toy.

"Hey, *babe*, can we talk for a second?" I asked her. In order to make Shane jealous, Tenley had to act as if she'd moved on. Right now, she was hanging on his every word with stars in her eyes, which was the complete opposite.

"Sure," Tenley said, and I could tell she was angry with me, but I seriously was trying to help her.

I pulled her away from the fire where the sand was cool and made your toes numb if you stood there too long without shoes on.

"Okay, the whole point of me being here is to show him that you've moved on and you're not giving him a second thought, so you're going to have to stop staring at him like you want to have his babies," I said. Tenley tried to argue with me, but I put my hand up.

"You can give him heart eyes all you want when you're back together." If that ever happened. I was extremely skeptical.

Tenley sighed and rubbed her forehead. "You're right. I know you're right. It's just hard to flip that switch."

"Just give me heart eyes," I said.

Tenley stared at me, squinting a little.

"You're giving me constipated eyes," I said, and she smacked my arm.

"Okay, how's this?" she asked, widening her eyes and pouting her lips a little.

"I think the point is that you're not supposed to try. It just happens," I said. "Let's try this." I touched the side of her face and put my hand on her waist, pulling her closer. Immediately, my breathing sped up, and so did hers. Tenley pressed up against me and set her hand on my shoulder. A moment ago, I'd been cold, but now it was like standing beside the fire.

"This-this works," she said, stuttering.

"I think we might be drawing some attention," I said, sensing people looking at us. I couldn't look away from her face to check.

"Should we try a kiss?" I asked.

"Yes," she breathed. Obviously, we had kissed before, but each time felt...monumental.

Tenley took the initiative and leaned forward, pressing her lips to mine. Fuck, she was a good kisser, I'd give her that. It was nice to be kissed, even if it wasn't real.

My thumb pressed into her cheek, pulling her closer so I could kiss her harder. Tenley's tongue licked the outside of my mouth and I let her in, meeting her halfway as she flicked a little greeting against my tongue. When Tenley kissed me there was no fumbling, no uncertainty, no wondering if you were doing it right. No second-guessing.

She was just that good.

Dimly, I heard people cheering behind us and Tenley broke the kiss, startled.

We both turned to see the group at the fire laughing and the guys hooting and making other suggestive noises. Of course. They still thought two women kissing was done entirely for the pleasure of men. Fuckers.

"Shane's looking," Tenley said, looking back at me with a smile.

"Good. That's what we wanted," I said, feeling hollow and wishing we could go back a few moments to the kiss.

"Let's go back to the fire. I'm cold," she said, pulling me closer to the group.

I went with her.

∽

THE NEXT HOUR WAS PAINFUL. Tenley had fully thrown herself into pretending to ignore Shane, while flirting with me and being charming and social with everyone else. My job was to smile and flirt back and pretend that I wasn't bothered by the whole thing. The reality of being a fake girlfriend was more difficult than I'd anticipated.

Shane tried a couple of times to draw Tenley into conversation, but she basically ignored him and kept laughing with her friends, or would just lean over and kiss me, making my head spin every time. She'd end the kiss and I'd be slammed back to reality that this beautiful girl kissing me was doing it to impress someone else.

As the night wore on and people got more and more drunk and reckless with the fire, all I wanted to do was go home and get in bed with a book for a while.

Tenley seemed completely oblivious, so I guess I was doing a good job at faking a smile. We sat together on a log of driftwood that functioned as a bench and she put her head on my shoulder with a sigh.

"Did you want to go soon?" she said, her voice a little dreamy as she stared into the fire.

I had wanted to leave hours ago. Once again, I had to ask myself why the hell I was doing this in the first place. And then Tenley looked up at me and smiled, making my heart thump.

It was long past time for me to accept the fact that I liked Tenley, even a little bit.

"Sure," I said. She put her arm around me and snuggled me closer to her. It might have been my imagination, but I thought I felt her lips in my hair.

"You smell good," she murmured, and I wished my heart would stop racing.

"Thanks," I said.

Tenley let out a sweet little noise that made me ache and then she stood up.

"I think we've done enough for tonight," she said, holding out her hand to help pull me up.

She yanked me, hard, so I crashed into her and we fell, both of us laughing.

"Sorry," she said.

"No you're not," I said. She had absolutely intended for that to happen.

"You're right, I'm not," she said, grinning. "Come on, let's go have some croissants."

I guess that was our post fake-date ritual now. Going back to Tenley's and having tea and croissants and talking about books. It had been a long time since the lobster dinner and there was no food at the beach, so I was starving.

"You did really good tonight," Tenley said when we got in the car. "I know you don't have to do this for me, and I'm still not really sure why you are, but thank you."

I nodded, fiddling with my seatbelt. "Yeah, of course. Guess I just felt like doing a good deed. Make up for all my bad ones." Not that I really had any, but she didn't know that.

"How bad have you been, Mia?" Tenley asked, the flirt still in her voice, even though there was no one else around.

I could put a stop to it, but I didn't.

"Wouldn't you like to know?" I said, leaning back in my seat and looking over at her.

"It's always the sweet ones that you have to watch out for," she said, backing out of the parking space and driving back to her house for tea and croissants and book talk into the wee hours of the morning.

~

WHEN I FINALLY FORCED MYSELF TO go home and get in bed, I couldn't stop thinking about Tenley. Thinking about her lips on mine. Thinking about how she'd felt next to me on the driftwood. I missed being with someone. It hadn't struck me until recently how much I longed for romantic companionship. My friends, especially Lark, were wonderful, but I wanted someone to share everything with. To snuggle in bed with. For sex, yes, but also for silliness and sick days and sunsets.

Once everything was done with Tenley, I was going to give dating a try again. I'd been on the apps before but hadn't had much luck making a connection. Casual stuff wasn't what I was after. Hookups could be fun, and a great way to scratch that physical itch, but I wanted deep intimacy.

Sometimes I thought about Sydney, who was so determined that she was never going to fall in love and was absolutely happy with her hookups, and then she let Lark move in and that was it. She didn't fall in love so much as was dragged kicking and screaming toward it.

Could something like that happen for me?

I wasn't sure.

What I did know was that I eventually gave up trying not to think of Tenley and got out my favorite vibrator to take care of it. Three times.

Chapter Six

OVER THE FOLLOWING WEEK, Tenley and I sort of settled into a comfortable routine. She would tease me at work, sometimes asking for a kiss. Sometimes I'd give it to her. She'd hang with me on my breaks and we'd have lunch together too. Hanging out with her felt an awful lot like dating, and I had to keep reminding myself that it wasn't real. I was only doing this until she got back with Shane and then she wouldn't be hanging out with me at lunch. She'd be calling him and making me sick by telling him how much she loved him.

Most of the time, Tenley didn't talk about Shane. Sometimes I would hear her almost bring him up, and then she'd stop herself. I appreciated it, but Shane was always there, hanging over my head like some kind of jock ghost. I hated it.

On Saturday I went over to Ingrid's to work on some more orders and I finally poured a practice piece for my new mold. After it cured and I removed it from the mold and made sure it looked good, I could take some pictures and add it to my store. I checked on some new glowing reviews on my site and couldn't stop the rush of satisfaction that I had. There was something so powerful about making something that helped someone else have an orgasm. It was a huge rush. The thank you emails I got from some of my customers were graphic, but I didn't mind. I was happy to help.

I had dinner with Ingrid and Athena before going home and putting on my outfit for the party. The night was chilly, so I put on jeans and a sweatshirt in case I got cold but had a cute top on underneath if I got warm.

Tenley didn't answer the door right away when I knocked so I waited. The door flew open and she was in the middle of brushing her teeth.

"Sorry, running late," she said around the toothbrush. Or at least that was what I thought she said.

Tenley dashed back to the bathroom as toothpaste dribbled down her chin and I told her I was just going to hang in her living room. I'd also brought the book back to return to her in pristine condition. As a thank you, I'd slipped one of my nicer bookmarks in between the pages.

While I waited, I looked at her shelves again, getting a better idea of her reading tastes. It didn't take a lot of looking to realize that she had a lot of romance. Like, a lot, and in a range of genres. It also didn't escape my notice that she had quite a collection of sapphic romances. And erotica. That was extremely interesting.

"I'm ready, I'm ready," Tenley said, rushing back into the room. She wore a t-shirt and joggers and had a plaid shacket slung over her arm. Her hair was pulled up and her fingers were stacked with gold rings.

"It's not like there's a definitive start time," I said. Those kinds of parties never had a set start time.

"Okay, let's go," she said, slipping her shacket on.

"I brought your book back," I said, holding it up and setting it on one of the tables.

"Great, thanks. I'll inspect it later and determine if I can lend you another book," she said, grabbing her bag.

"I think you'll be pleased," I said, twirling my keys on my finger. This time I was driving. I'd mostly agreed because I thought Tenley was going to want to go a little wild tonight.

I'd done a quick clean of my car before coming over, but Tenley hopped into the passenger seat without a comment about my shabby car. It got me where I needed to go and was a beast in the snow. Not much to look at, but she did her job.

Tenley leaned back in her seat and sighed. For a second, I considered telling her that we didn't have to go to the party. We could just keep driving. Go to Castleton and hit the bar. Or go back to her house and talk about books all night.

Instead, I clenched the steering wheel and kept driving to Tommy Webb's house.

～

THE PARTY WAS in full swing when we got there, and I could tell Tenley was excited.

"I'm going to see if I can talk to Shane," she said. "Maybe go get a drink or something. I'll be right back."

I could hear the desperation in her voice and it almost made me sad for her.

"Fine," I said, heading for the table of booze. The same people were here as last time and a few said hello and tried to exchange small talk with me, which was fine. I scanned the room as I grabbed a hard seltzer that I planned on drinking slowly since I was driving.

Tenley was in a corner with Shane, leaning against the wall and laughing at something he was saying. Guess she didn't even need me tonight. Shane was smiling down at her and it was obvious to anyone around them that they had chemistry. History.

Shane leaned down to say something in her ear and she

blushed and leaned into him. I wondered where Cassie was. She also hadn't been at the beach party last week.

"I can't believe they're not together anymore," someone said beside me. It was Karissa, one of Tenley's friends, and the one I disliked the least. She got points for having cool hair that was dyed half-blonde and half-brown, with split-color bangs that worked for her. She also seemed like kind of an outsider in the friend group. Like she didn't exactly fit in, but she didn't know where else to go. I could understand that.

"Oh, sorry," she said, realizing that she was talking to Tenley's "girlfriend."

"It's fine. I'm secure in my relationship," I said. I was very secure in this fake relationship.

"That's amazing. If I saw my girlfriend talking to her ex, I'd claw his eyes out," she said, and I started liking her more.

"Girlfriend?" I asked. I'd thought this was a no-queer party.

"Girlfriend, boyfriend, theyfriend, partner, whatever. I'd be fighting," she said, and I stared at her for a second. Karissa was rapidly gaining points here.

"They were together for a long time," I said as Tenley jokingly punched Shane's arm. He pulled out his phone and showed her something else that made her laugh.

"Anyway, I'd keep my eye on those two unless you want to date him too. I'm not judging," she said.

"Mmm, definitely not," I said. "He's not my type."

"Me neither. My taste in guys is the more frail they are, the more I want them. Like, if they look like they have a Victorian wasting disease and have been living in a garret? That does it for me."

I burst into unexpected laughter. I couldn't remember much about Karissa from high school, but she was funny as hell.

"Go get your girl," she said, nodding at Shane and Tenley.

"Rescue her from having to hear about his new paleo diet." Karissa rolled her eyes.

"Thanks for the tip," I said, reluctantly heading over to Tenley and Shane. My whole purpose in being here was to get them together like this, so it felt wrong to bust them up, but also, I wouldn't be a good fake girlfriend if I let her flirt with him all night in front of everyone.

"Hey, *babe*," I said, going up to Tenley with much more confidence than I felt.

"Oh, hey," Tenley said, her face falling. Wow, I didn't know I was such a disappointment. Why was I putting up with this?

"Can we talk for a second?" I asked through clenched teeth.

"Sure," she said, throwing a smile at Shane.

"I'll be right back."

I took her hand this time, but I clenched her fingers so hard she winced. Since I didn't want to go into Tommy's disgusting hovel of a home, I pulled her toward the back of the house and up the steps of the porch. There were a few rotting lawn chairs that I avoided and instead leaned on the porch railing.

Tenley yanked her hand back and inspected her fingers.

"What the hell, Mia? I swear you broke my hand," she said, glaring at me.

"Sorry, *babe*," I said. "But I wouldn't be a good fake girlfriend if I stood by and let you flirt with your ex in front of me for an hour."

"We weren't flirting for an hour," she said. "And your whole purpose of being here is to make Shane jealous, so it worked. Congratulations. Now can I go back and talk to him?"

My mouth dropped open. "Okay, wow, fuck you, Tenley."

She stared at me. "This is literally what we talked about! You'd help me get back with Shane. Now he's talking to me again, so what are you so mad about?"

I wanted to protest, but I couldn't. This was what I'd agreed to. So why did it hurt so fucking much?

"You're right," I said with a sigh. "You're right. Why don't you go back and see Shane. I'm just going to…sit here." It was cold, but at least I didn't have to talk to anyone.

"Are you sure?" At least she was hesitating.

"Yeah," I said. "Go flirt with your man." Ugh, saying that made me want to gag.

"I just…thank you," she said, hugging me out of the blue. "Thank you."

I inhaled the scent of her hair and she let me go.

"You're welcome," I said after she'd gone back into the barn.

~

I LASTED about ten minutes outside and then figured I should just go to my car. I messaged Lark to let her know that I was killing it as a fake girlfriend.

You should have made her pay you she sent.

Yeah, in hindsight I should have I responded. Money might make me feel a little bit better about this whole situation.

Another message came in, this one from Tenley.

I'm going home with Shane, so I don't need you to drive me. Thank you, THANK YOU! she sent.

I could feel the sincerity in her words, but I still felt empty. What else was there to do? I sure as hell wasn't going to go back into the party. It seemed as if my short stint as a fake girlfriend was officially over.

~

LARK AND SYDNEY were still up when I got back, and I didn't want to be alone, so I headed for their door and knocked before walking in.

"Hey," I said. Lark was plucking at her guitar and Sydney had a book in her hands.

"Hey, you okay?" Lark said, setting her guitar on the floor.

"Yeah, I'm fine," I said, leaning down to pet Clementine before taking a seat in their squishy chair. "Tenley went home with Shane, so that's over."

"You seem sad," Lark said. "You going to miss being a fake girlfriend?"

I tried to laugh, but it didn't really work.

"I need a real girlfriend," I said. "That's the solution."

"I think that's a great idea," Lark said. "Any candidates in mind?"

I shook my head. "Not really." Talking with Karissa and finding out she was queer was a pleasant surprise, but she wasn't really my type and I hadn't felt that attraction.

"Love, do you know of anyone?" Lark said, poking Sydney, who was completely absorbed in her book.

"Huh?" she said, blinking at us.

"Do you know anyone we could set our beautiful Mia up with?" Lark asked.

"Hmm," Sydney said, putting her finger in her book to mark her place. "What are you looking for?"

Wasn't that the question?

"I…don't know," I said, feeling silly. "I've never really known what my type is. I just sort of see who I'm attracted to and then go for it. My exes have all been pretty different from each other."

"Would you date someone who lives outside of Arrowbridge?" Sydney asked.

"Of course. I feel like all the people I would have dated moved away to other places. Even though Arrowbridge is super queer now, it's not like there's tons of jobs to lure people back," I said.

"Isn't that the truth?" Lark said.

"Should have been born into a family business," Sydney said, and Lark threw a pillow at her.

"Nepotism is not an economic solution!" Lark said.

"It is for some people," Sydney said, smirking. Looking at the lives of the people in power, Sydney wasn't wrong, per se.

"Going back to Mia," Lark said, yanking the pillow back from Sydney, "we will be on the lookout and will put out the lesbian bat signal that you're single and ready to mingle."

I made a face. "Please don't make me sound so desperate."

"We're not making you sound desperate. Just…available," Lark said.

"That sounds desperate," I said.

∽

TENLEY DIDN'T SEND me any more messages that night, and I couldn't stop thinking about what she was doing with Shane. They were probably fucking right now. Maybe he was really good at sex to make up for his awful personality.

Yeah, I had doubts.

No matter what I did to distract myself, my brain kept hitting play on images and scenes of what Shane and Tenley would look like fucking. Would she come? Did he know how to make that happen for her? Would she fake it to protect his ego? Or would she show and tell him exactly what she needed? Tenley didn't seem like the kind of person who would be meek in any area of her life, but you never knew what someone was like in bed until you were in it with them.

I didn't fall asleep for hours.

Chapter Seven

SINCE I DIDN'T GET much sleep on Saturday night, I was dragging on Sunday, but it was the day of Layne's barbecue and I wasn't going to miss it. More than seeing my friends, I needed to get out of my own head for a while. Plus, there would be amazing food.

Sydney and Lark asked if I wanted to ride with them, but I decided to take my own car so I could leave when I wanted. I also needed to get some stuff at the grocery store after.

I'd been to the house before, but it still shocked me when I pulled into the driveway. It was an insult to call it a house. This place was a mansion. The kind of place I'd browse the listing for in the middle of the night and tell myself I could never fucking afford it. Not that I would want to. Way too many rooms, but I didn't hate the pool.

Since I'd been firmly informed that I shouldn't bring anything, I felt a little strange showing up without any kind of gift, but I was greeted with cheers and hugs.

The house was owned by the family Layne worked for, but they were away on a family vacation without Layne, so we had the place to ourselves, and we didn't have to worry that one of the twin girls she looked after was going to be eavesdropping on our conversation.

Layne shoved a plate in my hand and Honor asked what I wanted to drink, and I felt myself relaxing and brushing off the bad vibes of the night before.

Once I had food and drinks, I found a seat near Joy and her girlfriend, Ezra. I hadn't talked much with Ezra, but she was one of those people I'd determined that I wanted to be friends with. Not only was she super sex-positive, she was also a sex toy reviewer and she was going to school in the fall to become a sex therapist. Our brains were definitely in sync.

"I'm sorry," Joy said, putting her hand on my arm. "Lark and Sydney told us about your girlfriend." While I had told Sydney and Lark that my relationship with Tenley was fake, no one else knew that it was.

"Oh, yeah, thanks," I said, feeling my face go red. I gulped my drink so I wouldn't have to look at the sympathy in Joy's eyes. She worked at the bookstore and ran book club and was one of the sweetest people I'd ever met. Not to mention she was incredible at finding the exact book you didn't know you needed.

"Breakups can be hard," Ezra said. I'd noticed that she tended to be quiet around new people, so I assumed that she might need a little time to warm up, but I couldn't wait to talk with her about sex toys. I was curious to see what trends she noticed lately that I might be able to incorporate into my business. There was almost nothing I loved more than talking shop with other people who were in the same industry. There were a few people online that also had shops that I'd made friendships with but having someone living so close was on another level.

Of course, I'd have to actually tell her about my side hustle for us to talk about it, and I hadn't gotten up the courage to do that yet. Maybe after another drink.

I also noticed that Sydney's pink-haired employee, Everly,

was here with her girlfriend, Ryan, taking care of all the grilling. They laughed together and it was nice to see Everly having a good time. She had social anxiety, so parties like this could be hard for her. No one judged her for it, or thought any less of her, but she still usually needed a breather, or to go home early. Her girlfriend, Ryan, was incredibly tall, buff, and totally intimidating. She was also the homeowner's niece. Ryan was one of those people that I didn't know how to talk to, so I just kind of kept my focus on Everly.

There were some other people here I recognized, including Kendra, who owned Mainely Books, and her chiseled, redheaded girlfriend, Theo, who was talking animatedly to another couple, Hayden and Alessi. The fact that the party was entirely made up of queer people meant the energy was the opposite of the barn party I'd gone to. I shuddered thinking about it.

What was Tenley doing right now? Had she woken up in Shane's bed this morning? Had she gotten up and made him breakfast? Had he made her breakfast? Was she happy?

I had to stop myself from sending her a message to ask if she'd gotten off last night. Not only was it none of my business, it was kind of tacky.

"Mia, you there?" Lark asked, sitting down on my other side with two plates full of food while Sydney carried their drinks.

"Yeah, just ruminating," I said.

"Ohh, that's a good word," Lark said. "I wonder if I could fit that in a song lyric."

"I'd love to hear you try," I said.

"You did bring your guitar, love," Sydney said. "I know everyone here would like it if you sang."

Lark blushed and handed Sydney her plate. "Maybe later. I'd need another drink first."

"You can have whatever you want," Sydney said, giving her a kiss.

"Yes I can," Lark said, twirling one of Sydney's dark curls around her finger.

The only, and I mean only, downside to this barbecue was that it was majority couples. Very in-love couples. Couples that couldn't keep their hands off each other. You could practically see the clouds of love all around, like smoke. I hoped some of it rubbed off on me and made me attract someone new.

It was a good idea for me to have a new crush. I hadn't had one in a while, so I was definitely overdue. Crushes were fun. Crushes were easy. I was absolutely ready to be crushed a little.

"Joy-Joy, do you know anyone we can set Mia up with?" Sydney asked, leaning across the chairs.

"Oh, I'm not sure. What's your type?" There was that question again.

"I don't know," I said, raising my hands in defeat. "I have to meet the person to judge. Sorry that's not helpful."

Joy wasn't deterred. "Don't worry. I will keep my eye out and I'll put out some feelers through Kendra to see if there's anyone in Castleton that she thinks would be good for you." Kendra's girlfriend was hot as hell, so I trusted her judgment.

"Just don't make me sound too desperate," I said. "Please."

Joy squeezed my arm. "Don't worry, we'll find your princess."

"You just want everyone to be happy," Ezra said, pulling Joy over for a kiss.

"Maybe I do and maybe I do," Joy said, laughing.

"Hey, Skylar Alyssa!" Sydney yelled and both Alessi and Hayden turned around from where they'd been getting food. "When is your next book out because I have a *need*."

Alessi, who was also known as the sapphic romance author Skylar Alyssa, gave her plate to Hayden and walked over.

"It's proving to be a little challenging, but it's coming, I promise. Just a little slower than I'd like," she said, frowning.

"That's got to be so hard, I don't know how you do it," Sydney said, shaking her head.

"The only thing I've ever tried writing is fanfic, and it wasn't very good," Joy said, her cheeks going a little pink.

"Wait, what was your ship?" I asked.

She gave me a sad look. "Clexa."

"Ouch," I said. "But at least you get to write a happy ending in fanfic?"

"It doesn't make up for what happened in the show," she said, and I couldn't help but agree.

It didn't matter that the show had been on years ago, your ship not sailing still hurt.

"If we were a ship, what would our name be?" Lark asked Sydney.

"Slark? Sydark?" Sydney suggested.

"We could be Jez," Joy said.

Everyone joined in making ship names for all the couples and there was a tight feeling in my chest. I wanted a ship name. I wanted a person to have a ship name with.

At some point a few people hopped into the pool to cool off and I decided to make my move with Ezra. Joy was deep in a conversation with Alessi about a potential book event.

"Are you excited about going back to school?" I asked her, hoping that wasn't too boring of a question.

"I'm nervous. It's been a few years," she said. "I'm trying not to think about the cost, or the time commitment."

I felt like I was still recovering from graduating school. At least once a week I had a nightmare that I'd forgotten about signing up for a class and was sitting in the final exam without having gone to any classes.

"Are you still doing toy reviews and so forth?" I asked.

"I'm going to try to keep up, and keep writing my advice

column, but I won't know if I can juggle everything until the fall," she said. This was my chance. I scooted closer and dropped my voice.

"So, um, I actually have an online store where I make silicone toys," I said, pulling up my website on my phone and showing it to her.

Ezra looked at the phone and then at me and smiled.

"It's incredible how accessible toys are these days," she said.

"I know. I kind of did it on a whim and got addicted to designing them and coming up with cool color combinations. I don't do anything too creative, but eventually I'd love to have my own space to really go wild," I said.

"If you want, I'd be happy to do an honest review for you," Ezra said.

"Oh that's okay. I'm still really new at this," I said. One thing that was keeping me from really expanding was that I kept my prices low. Not that I wasn't putting all my effort into making the best product I could, but I was one person in a garage. I didn't have the hardcore equipment or years of experience or a freaking engineering or chemistry degree like some people. I was just a girl in a garage with some silicone and glitter and some tentacle toy molds.

"We all have to start somewhere. Don't downplay your skills," she said.

"Thanks. I just…I don't tell people about it for fear they'd get weird and judgmental," I said.

Ezra rolled her eyes. "Tell me about it. I can't wait to tell people I'm a certified sex therapist and watch their heads explode."

We both laughed and talked about weird reactions people had given us to our passions until Joy came back and asked Ezra if she wanted another drink.

"I'm good, thanks," she said, reaching out to take Joy's

hand and press a kiss to her palm. Joy blushed and grinned down at Ezra.

"Do you need anything, Mia?" Joy asked me.

"Just some water would be great, if it's not a big deal," I said.

"Of course, be right back." Joy took drink orders from a few other people and went off to get them.

"I tell her she doesn't have to do that, but I'm fighting a losing battle. It's easier to just let her," Ezra said, watching Joy with love in her eyes. She also had the word inked across her knuckles, which was totally badass.

Joy came back with a tray of drinks and I took my water and thanked her.

Layne was also coming around with more food, and Ryan was still at the grill, making fruit kebabs that smelled so good, I could barely stop myself from drooling.

I grabbed a few and lay back in my chair.

"I'm guessing this is much better than the barn party from last night," Lark said.

"Ten thousand times better," I said. Last night had been awful.

"Have you heard anything from her?" she asked in a low voice.

"No," I said before biting a piece of grilled pineapple that burst in my mouth. Fuck, that was good. Everly had drizzled each kebab with lime juice and hot honey that got all over my fingers.

"Are you going to say anything? Do you think she'll be at CG tomorrow?" Lark asked.

"I have no idea," I said. "I'm sure she's too busy with Shane to be thinking about me."

Lark had a look on her face like she wanted to comment.

"Go ahead. Say 'I told you so.'"

She leaned over and stole another bite of pineapple from my plate.

"Good friends never say 'I told you so,' and I really didn't know how this was going to shake out. I'm sorry that you're sad."

"Thank you," I said. "I'll get over it."

∼

I LEFT the party a while later with a full belly, but still with that hollow feeling I'd had since last night after the party.

I could message Tenley. I could. It would be easy. I could check in and see how she was doing. But then she might tell me, and I didn't want to know. I didn't want to hear about how wonderful Shane was. I was never going to think he was wonderful.

When I got home after buying a few groceries, I took a shower and put on my most comfortable pajamas before snuggling into bed with one of my favorite series that was basically The Little Mermaid, but sapphic. The princess in this case was a sexy, ripped butch that was always trying to find her moral compass. Talk about swoonworthy.

I'd just gotten through the first chapter when I heard a knock at my door. It was late, but I assumed it was probably just Lark coming over for a gossip session or maybe because she needed something.

I got up and shuffled to the door. I didn't have a peephole, but I didn't really need one. It wasn't like anyone other than Lark or Sydney ever knocked on it.

I didn't find Sydney or Lark on the other side of the door when I opened it.

No, it was Tenley, and she was a mess.

"Can I come in?" she said through sobs.

"Yeah, of course," I said, stunned for a second. This was completely unexpected.

Tenley sniffed hard and walked in. She wasn't even wearing shoes. Just socks.

"How did you get here?" I asked.

"I drove," she said in a robotic voice as she stared into nothing, tears still running down her cheeks. It was lucky that she'd gotten here in one piece, given how she looked.

"Do you want some coffee or something?"

She shrugged one shoulder and continued to stare and cry. Okay. Looked like I needed to take matters into my own hands. I guided her over to the couch and pushed on her shoulders until she sat down. I ran to grab tissues from the bathroom and then went to make some coffee. Having caffeine this late at night was going to fuck everything up for tomorrow, but this seemed like an emergency.

Once I had the coffee brewed, I added some vanilla syrup and almond milk because I knew that was the way Tenley liked it.

"What happened?" I asked gently as I sat down next to her and held out the cup of coffee. She took it in both hands, gripping it tight.

"Shane broke up with me. Again." I assumed as much, but I waited for her to continue.

"He, um," she said, sniffing and then taking a sip of coffee, "we went to his place together and I thought everything was fine. We had sex and then I made him breakfast and he said he had stuff to do so I went home. He was gone for hours and I was freaking out. I couldn't get a hold of him and finally he messaged me back and said that he didn't want to be with me anymore and that we were definitely done." Her voice broke and she sobbed.

This turn of events was absolutely predictable, but that

didn't mean it was right. I ripped a fresh tissue out of the box and handed it to her.

"Tenley, I'm so sorry," I said.

"Thanks. But I know you want to say that you saw this coming. It's written all over your face."

Oops. I thought I'd been hiding my emotions well.

"I am sorry. I truly am. You don't deserve this. Any of it." My voice was sharp, and I reached out and put my hand on her leg so she would believe me.

"Why do I love him?" she asked, and I took the cup of coffee away from her and pulled her into a hug.

"I don't think anyone has figured out the formula on love yet," I said.

"I don't want to love him anymore," she whispered into my shoulder.

"I know," I said. "You won't love him like this forever." On some level, she probably always would. Wasn't that the thing about first loves? That they stayed with you for the rest of your life, even if you'd moved on.

"I don't want to feel like this," she said, sniffing, and I just kept holding her.

Chapter Eight

EVENTUALLY TENLEY RAN out of tears and went to the bathroom to wash her face and blow her nose again. When she came back out, she tried to give me a smile.

"I hate that you keep seeing me like this," she said, gesturing at her face. "No one sees me like this."

"That's what fake girlfriends are for," I said.

"You don't have to do that anymore, Mia," she said. "You don't owe me anything. I owe you a hell of a lot more than a favor at this point. God, I'm so sorry I dragged you into this." She took her hair out of the messy bun and tried to run her fingers through it, but everything was so tangled that she gave up. She let out a frustrated sound and I went and got her a hairbrush.

"Here," I said.

"Stop taking care of me," she said, but she took the brush and started working it through her hair.

"It's kind of hard to stop taking care of you when you're the one who ended up at my apartment in the middle of the night after a breakup," I said.

"I didn't know where else to go," she said. "I didn't even

think about where I was going until I realized I was pulling into the parking lot."

She'd only been here one other time to pick me up, so it was kind of a surprise that she remembered I lived here. True, it was on the main street of Arrowbridge, but I couldn't help but be touched that she came to me.

"Your friends wouldn't have given you tissues and coffee and a hairbrush?" I asked.

"They would have, but they also would have talked my ear off and told me that Shane would come back, that he was a good guy, that we were meant to be together and so forth," she said. "I didn't want to hear any of that. I feel like shit and I don't need to feel shittier."

"What do you want right now?" I asked.

Tenley thought about that for a few moments.

"I want to scream, and I want to get drunk and then pass out," she said.

I nodded. "I think we can handle that."

∼

FIRST, I gave her a pillow to scream into as long as she wanted, then I got out a bottle of wine because I didn't seem to have anything else in the house. She said that was fine, as long as I had another bottle, and I did.

Not wanting her to drink alone, I poured a glass for myself and held it up.

"To forgetting?" I asked.

"Definitely," she said, and we tapped our glasses together.

Tenley downed her first glass without even taking a breath and held it out to me to fill up again.

"Okay, then," I said, handing it to her when it was full. She chugged that one too and held it out again.

"Before you have another one, let's have some water," I said and she frowned at me but didn't protest.

I poured her a glass of water and made her down it before she went for that third glass of wine. The bottle was just about empty, so I was going to have to open another, but she needed to pace herself.

"Fuck Shane!" Tenley said. Good. I'd been hoping she was moving toward the anger stage. Being mad at him was good. He deserved it. I hadn't fantasized about beating someone else up since high school, but if I saw Shane? I might not be able to stop myself from giving him several kicks in the family jewels.

"Fuck Shane," I agreed.

"His balls always smelled," she said, and it was a good thing I hadn't been drinking or else I would have sprayed liquid everywhere.

"Jesus, Tenley. I didn't need to know that," I said, cringing. I didn't want to know anything about any part of Shane's anatomy.

"Sometimes I'd get in the shower with him and like, wash them for him," she continued as if I hadn't said anything. The wine seemed to be having an effect.

"Tenley, I am begging you. Please stop talking about Shane's balls."

"He hates oral sex too. Well, doing it on me. But he needs a blow job every day or else he doesn't feel like 'himself.'" She used air quotes around the last word.

"Jesus Fucking Christ, Tenley, I don't need to know this! Stop talking about it!" I put my hands over my ears like a child, but I didn't know what else to do.

Tenley started cackling and I knew the wine had absolutely kicked in.

Now that Tenley was talking about Shane, it was like when she got talking about books.

I learned a lot of things about Shane from Tenley. So much

more than I ever wanted or needed to. By the time she finally slowed down, I was exhausted.

Tenley snuggled into the couch and sighed.

"Can I stay here?" she asked.

"Yeah, you can stay here," I said. "Do you want a change of clothes or anything?"

Tenley closed her eyes for a second. "I would love a shower."

"Sure, go for it. I can grab you some pajamas and a fresh towel," I said, getting up. Tenley reached out and grabbed my hand.

"Thank you for putting up with me," she said, yawning.

"You're welcome," I said, looking down into her eyes.

"I liked being your fake girlfriend," she said, her words slurring together a little bit.

I turned and went to get the clothes and her towel. "I liked being your fake girlfriend, too," I said, but she didn't hear me.

～

TENLEY TOOK a quick shower and emerged warm and sleepy. I'd made up a bed for her on the couch and she lay down with a happy sigh.

"Night night, fake girlfriend," she said before shutting her eyes. I tucked her in and made sure her phone was plugged in to charge before I said "goodnight, Tenley," and headed to bed myself.

I didn't sleep for a long time.

～

WHEN I WOKE up the next morning, I was startled because I heard someone in the bathroom. For a second, I was terrified that someone had broken into my house, but then I remembered Tenley coming over last night.

Tenley had spent the night and slept on my couch. How strange was that? I hadn't even had a warning that she was coming over so I could make sure everything was clean. I guess that didn't matter now. She wasn't going to be worrying about the cleanliness in my house when her fucking heart was shattered.

I rolled out of bed and peeked through the doorway. Tenley was coming back from the bathroom, her eyes half closed and her hair absolutely everywhere.

"Mmm," she croaked at me, lazily waving one hand before she slumped back onto the couch, pulling the blanket up over her head.

"Hey," I said, sitting down on the couch next to her.

"Mmm," she said, her voice muffled under the blanket.

"Can I get you anything?" I asked, my own voice rough. I felt like garbage and I needed coffee and food very soon.

"Ughhhhhh," she said.

"I'm going to make some coffee and breakfast. I have croissants and eggs and frozen breakfast burritos and strawberries," I said, mentally going through my fridge and freezer.

Tenley pulled the blanket back down and blinked at me.

"Okay," she said. Immediately I made her a cup of coffee, a glass of water, and heated up a croissant for her to nibble on while I made some quick scrambled eggs and sliced some strawberries.

Tenley ate the croissant slowly, pulling it apart in tiny bits, shoving them cautiously into her mouth.

"How are you feeling?" I asked, keeping my voice low.

"Like shit," she croaked.

"Understandable," I said. "Do you need anything for pain?"

"Sure," she said. I grabbed her some pain pills and slid two into her hand.

Tenley swallowed them down with a grimace and a sip of water.

"Did you want any eggs?" I asked.

"Not yet. I'm going to see if this stays down and then I'll try again," she said, sitting back and closing her eyes.

"I'll keep a plate warm for you," I said, munching on a strawberry.

"Fuck, Mia. What is happening to my life?" she said, as tears slipped down her face.

"It's okay," I said, touching her foot.

"It's not. It's absolutely not okay right now. Fuck."

I handed her more tissues as she sniffled. I finished my breakfast and she cried softly. I just gave her time and didn't try to offer too many words of comfort. I could tell she didn't want them. All she needed right now was a few minutes to get herself together.

I took the dishes to the kitchen and Tenley slowly got up from the couch and went to the bathroom.

When she came back out, her face was freshly washed, and she wasn't crying anymore.

"Sorry for wrecking your Sunday," she said, sitting back on the couch.

"You didn't wreck my Sunday," I said, closing the dishwasher and rejoining her on the couch.

"What did you have planned?" she asked.

My original plan was to go over to Ingrid's and do some work, but I wasn't going to mention the work part.

"Going over to see my sister," I said. "But it's fine. I see her all the time. I have to pick up my niece from daycare at least once a week anyway, so I'll see her a lot." I could also squeeze in a few hours of work time, if I had enough energy.

"I'm sorry," she said. "I feel like all I do is apologize to you. I hate it."

"The next time I have a messy breakdown, I'll call you," I said. "You can come over and play with my hair and bring me ice cream."

"Is that what you do when you have a breakdown?" she asked.

"I mean, under ideal circumstances. Oh, and cupcakes. I definitely need breakdown cupcakes."

Tenley laughed. "I kind of like the idea of breakdown cupcakes. What flavor would they be?"

"Oh, I think most breakdowns require chocolate," I said.

Tenley nodded. "That makes complete sense. Shit, now I want a cupcake for later."

"Hold that thought," I said, getting up and going to the kitchen cabinets. "Tenley, you're in luck. We can make some breakdown cupcakes," I said, holding up a box of cake mix I'd been saving for PMS baking.

"Fuck yes, I'm in," she said. "Once I'm sure that I won't throw up."

"Yeah, let's give it a little while," I said, shuddering.

～

TENLEY DIDN'T SEEM to want to talk about the previous night, so I turned on the TV and let her put on whatever she wanted. She picked a silly reality show that both of us had seen before, but she started back at the beginning.

"I am trash for this show," she said. "I love seeing other people having drama that doesn't involve me."

"Truth," I said. My regular life was pretty drama-free, thankfully. It sounded like Tenley's wasn't, between everything with Shane and then her family stuff.

We laughed together and talked about our theories on the

motivations of the people and Tenley seemed like she was perking up.

"Okay, I think I'm good to make breakdown cupcakes now," she said, standing up.

She wore my pajamas, and while they didn't fit (they were a little baggy), she looked good in them.

Tenley went right into the kitchen and started pulling things out of the fridge and asking me where the large bowls were and if I had a mixer. I didn't bake a ton, but I did have enough supplies to make cupcakes. I even had a can of strawberry frosting that we could use.

"We can put fresh strawberries in the center of the cupcakes," Tenley suggested, and I thought that was a perfect idea.

The kitchen was a small area, so we kept bumping into each other, but I didn't mind and neither did Tenley. Her eyes were brighter, and she was even humming a little to herself when she mixed the batter together and I sliced strawberries for the center of the cupcakes.

We got everything in the cupcake pan and in the oven with minimal fuss and I put all the dishes in the dishwasher and turned it on.

Tenley's phone went off and she read the message with a frown.

"Guess Shane has told everyone we broke up. Again," she said in a monotone voice. Tenley put her phone on silent and put it with the screen facing down on the counter.

"I can't wait for my brothers to give me even more shit," she said, rubbing her eyes.

"Hey," I said, touching her shoulder. "You don't have to think about that right now. This is a safe space," I said, gesturing at my tiny apartment.

"I wish it was," she said. "I sometimes think about what would have happened if I'd moved away after college. If I'd picked a random city and gone there with nothing to start a new life."

She pulled herself up until she was sitting on the counter with her bare feet swinging back and forth.

"I think about that too," I said. "I always used to say when I was growing up that I wouldn't be caught dead here after college. I was going to move far away and only come back on holidays. And then reality gave me a nice slap in the face." College had left me completely beyond broke, and that had also been when my sister had decided she wanted to have a baby. I'd been living with my parents, but we basically were ships passing in the night, so I spent all my time over at Ingrid's and learned really quick how to give her hormone injections and way more details about pregnancy than I wanted to. Guess it might come in handy later in life.

Right around the same time I knew it was time to get my own place, my parents said they were putting up the house for sale and moving to France Everything had worked out perfectly in the end. Sure, Arrowbridge wasn't an awesome queer-friendly city with a great lesbian bar, but I had book club, didn't I? And Lark and Sydney down the hall. If I got into a bind, I had people I could call that would come and lend me a hand. If I moved to another place, I'd have to completely start over and build all new relationships. Plus, then I wouldn't be able to make my toys in my sister's garage every weekend.

"Life is strange that way," she said. "You picture how it's going to be and then it's nothing like that."

"I definitely didn't plan on being someone's fake girlfriend," I said.

"I didn't plan on fake dating a woman to try and get my ex to come back," she said, her lips lifting in a sad smile. "When I say it out loud, I can hear how completely silly it sounds. Why did I think that was going to work?" She met my eyes and I kept my mouth shut.

"No comment," I said.

Tenley threw her hands up in the air. "Then why did you go along with it?"

"You know, I've been asking myself that this entire time. I have no answer for you." I didn't know if I ever would.

Now would probably be a good time to tell her that I wasn't straight, but I couldn't force my mouth to say the words.

Tenley inhaled through her nose and shook her head. "I don't want to think about Shane anymore. He's out of my life and that's over. Done. Finished. Fuck him."

"Fuck him," I agreed. "I know it's only been a minute, but do you want to date? Have a rebound?"

Tenley made a face. "No idea. I'm going to see if I can get through a week without having at least two breakdowns a day and then we'll see."

I laughed. "That's probably smart. Rebounds can mess you up."

"You sound like you speak from personal experience," she said.

"Maybe a little bit," I said. My first girlfriend in college had absolutely wrecked me and I'd gone immediately out to find someone else so I didn't hurt all the time and then I'd fallen for her and gotten my heart broken twice in the space of a few months. Never again.

"We'll find you the right guy," she said.

"I'm good for now," I said.

To avoid talking about dating men, I started wiping down the counters, but Tenley was staring at me.

"What?" I asked.

"I'm trying to figure out your taste in guys so I can be on the lookout," she said.

"Tall," I said. "Tall guys are good. And, um, handsome."

Tenley snorted. "Obviously. But do you like more sensitive guys, or more sporty guys or what?"

"Uhhh, sensitive and sporty," I said.

"That can be a tough combination," Tenley said. "Plus, there's the fact that most of the guys around here you've known forever, and you know too much."

I shuddered. Even if I dated guys, I could never date someone from around here because of knowing too much. It was kind of hard to find a guy attractive when your friend had dated him and told you all the details of their sex life, down to all his extremely specific kinks.

Tenley sighed. "Guys are better in books anyway. They're always wearing gray sweatpants and leaning in doorways and brooding and saying the right things. Mmm."

I loved all of that stuff, just when women were doing it. Guys didn't have a monopoly on gray sweatpants and leaning. Fuck. What were we talking about?

The timer for the cupcakes finally went off and we got the tray out of the oven and set them on the stove to cool before we frosted them.

"I have some piping bags if we want to get fancy," I said.

"Fuck yeah, let's get fancy," Tenley said.

Before I put the frosting into the piping bags, I whipped some air into it to make it super fluffy. I handed a piping bag to Tenley. "Go for it."

I went for a simple design, just making little dots of frosting on the top, but Tenley was making what looked like a rose.

"Wow, you're good at that," I said.

"Thank you," she said, not looking up from what she was doing.

"Have you done this before?" I asked.

"I've dabbled in baking. I've dabbled in a lot of hobbies. I can't seem to find anything that sticks. I mean, other than reading," she said. "But now that I write books, I consider reading as part of my job."

She stood up and studied her handiwork.

"Not bad."

"You put me to shame," I said. Not that I was a terrible decorator, but Tenley's looked like a professional had done them. We split up the cupcakes and each decorated half. In the end, Tenley's looked much better than mine, but they tasted the same when you ate them.

I picked up a cupcake and peeled the paper off as Tenley did the same.

"Happy breakup," I said.

"Happy breakup to you too, former fake girlfriend," she said, and we toasted with our cupcakes.

"Strawberries were a good idea," I said as I took my first bite. The fresh strawberries were sweet and bright in contrast with the rich chocolate and then the strawberry frosting added a creaminess that brought it all together.

"Definitely," Tenley agreed, devouring her cupcake and then licking her fingers. "I think, in my vulnerable emotional state, that I need another cupcake."

I laughed. "Tenley, you can have as many cupcakes as you want."

She grinned and reached for another.

~

I KIND OF ASSUMED THAT once she had recovered from her hangover, Tenley would have gone home, but she didn't seem to want to leave. She kept nibbling at cupcakes and making more coffee and wandering around my apartment.

"This place is cute," she said.

"Cute means small," I said.

"I mean, it is small, but there's nothing wrong with that. Cleaning an entire house is a pain in the ass," she said. That was true. One of the rules growing up was that my sister and I were in charge of most of the cleaning and dragging a vacuum cleaner up and down the stairs was a task I never wanted to do again. Ingrid's house was all one level, which made things a little bit easier.

"Not a lot of room for books, though," I said.

"True. Sometimes I worry about the foundation, though." She flopped down on the couch with a sigh. She was still wearing my clothes.

"Hey, do you have a sweatshirt?" she asked.

"Yeah, sure," I said, wondering if she was cold. I pulled one out of the closet. It was from my college and all faded.

"Thanks," she said, pulling it over her head.

I joined her on the couch, and we gazed at each other for a moment. I looked away first, feeling nervous for some reason.

"You seem to be feeling better. I think the cupcakes were a success," I said.

"Definitely," she said through a yawn. "Do you mind if I take a quick nap?"

"No, go for it," I said as she snuggled down and pulled up the couch pillow to lay her head on.

Tenley curled her feet up and closed her eyes. I covered up her legs with a blanket and she cracked one eye open.

"Thanks," she said.

"You're welcome."

While Tenley slept, I tried to be as quiet as I could, picking up the apartment and cleaning the bathroom. She had completely crashed, so I sat on the couch next to her and scanned through my digital to-read list. Feeling a little naughty, I opened an extremely sexy age-gap romance set in a sex club that I'd been saving for a while. Tenley might have been asleep, but there was something fun about reading something so explicit with her right there. My body started to sweat and I could feel my cheeks heating up.

The blogger who recommended this book hadn't been lying about how sexy it was.

"What are you reading over there?" a voice said, and I almost screamed and simultaneously fell off the couch.

"Holy shit, Tenley," I said, putting my phone down and trying to get my heart rate back under control. "You scared me."

I looked over to find her with her eyes open and a sleepy expression on her face.

"How long have you been watching me, creep?"

She rolled her eyes and sat up. "I wasn't watching you. I woke up and you happened to be in my line of sight." I didn't exactly believe her, but I wasn't going to argue.

"So, what are you reading?" she asked, and my face went completely red.

"Nothing," I said.

"Uh huh," she said, stretching her arms over her head. She was still wearing my sweatshirt.

"I should probably get home," she said, running her fingers through her messy hair. "I've crashed with you long enough."

"It hasn't been that bad," I said. "I mean, the crying was a little intense, but that's not your fault. Anyone would be upset after a breakup. At least you didn't break the law or set anything on fire."

Tenley snorted as she stood up. "Don't think I didn't consider it. But if I burned down Shane's house then he'd be able to get the insurance money and I don't want that."

"And there's the getting caught part," I said.

Tenley gave me a wicked smile. "I wouldn't get caught."

She gathered the clothes she'd shown up to my house in and I put them in a bag for her.

"I'll wash this and give it back to you," she said.

"Take your time. Do you need some shoes?" I asked. Our feet weren't the same size, but I had some flip-flops that sort of worked that she put on.

"I know I've said it before, but seriously, Mia. Thank you. I don't take any of this lightly. You were there for me last night," she said as we stood together in the doorway.

"You're welcome, Tenley," I said, and she leaned closer to me just a little bit. Her lips parted as if she wanted to say something else.

"Really," she said. "Thank you."

"Okay, okay," I said, feeling weird about all the gratitude. "Get out of here, weirdo."

I might have said the words, but a part of me wanted to yank her back inside and shut the door and tell her that we could hang out for the rest of the weekend if she wanted. I could make more cupcakes and we could make dinner later and maybe have a moderate amount of wine compared to last night.

But I didn't. I watched her carefully walk down the stairs so she didn't trip in my flip-flops and then push through the door to go to her car.

She was gone and my apartment was way too empty.

Chapter Nine

Only an hour later, my phone buzzed with an incoming message.

I'm bored and I can't stop thinking about Shane. Come over Tenley sent. The message completely floored me. She wanted me to come over? Right now?

Give me thirty minutes I responded. I hopped in the shower, shaved, and washed and conditioned my hair before getting out and picking out something cute to wear. Not too cute. I didn't want her to think I was trying to impress her or anything. My white and green striped linen shirt and matching shorts were kinda gay, but I didn't think Tenley was going to clock that. I had much gayer outfits that I was going to avoid wearing around her. Like my GIRLS GAYS THEYS shirt. But I did put on my Protect Trans Kids shirt under the linen top. You didn't have to be queer to support trans kids, that was just the right thing to do.

My hair went into two low buns and I had to admit, I looked good. Not that it mattered. Tenley wasn't looking at me like that.

When I got to her house, I was a little nervous as I turned

off my car and got out. I'd seen her not that long ago, but things were different now. We didn't *have* to hang out. There was no purpose to me being here, other than she'd asked me to be and I'd agreed. I no longer owed her anything, yet here I was. She did have that impressive library, though. That was worth driving over for.

I knocked on the door and heard Tenley call out that I should come in. I did, slipping my shoes off and leaving them by the door.

"I'm in the kitchen," she called, and I headed toward the back of the house to find Tenley barefoot and wearing a flowered sundress as various pots steamed on the stove.

"Hey," she said, spinning around. "I'm making dinner. I should have asked you what you wanted or if you'd already eaten."

"I haven't," I said. I hadn't even considered that food would be involved. I'd been too worried about what I was going to wear.

"How do you feel about Greek pasta salad with orzo and honey balsamic chicken thighs?" she asked, turning off one of the burners.

"Sounds good to me," I said. Better than what I probably would have had at home. "Can I help?"

Tenley looked at me and bit her bottom lip. "This is going to sound mean, but I don't let people cook in my kitchen."

I laughed. "That doesn't sound mean. I can get the plates and set the table," I said.

"Thanks," Tenley said. "I'm just…I'm particular about cooking and it's easier to do it than have to show someone else how to do it."

How utterly adorable. I hadn't pictured Tenley as being kitchen strict. It made sense, though, with how many rules she had about me borrowing one of her books. I wondered if Shane had tried to bully her in the kitchen.

Probably not. Shane seemed like the kind of guy who would think cooking was beneath him, but who couldn't cook an egg if his life depended on it.

"We can eat in the living room if you want. The dining room is kind of a mess," she said, draining the pasta. "There are fold-up trays in the corner."

I took the plates to the living room and found several trays with legs that I set up in front of the couch. They were pretty handy, I had to admit. Better than putting everything on the coffee table or having to balance it in your lap.

"I need to get me a few of those trays," I said when I came back to get silverware and glasses and bowls for the pasta salad.

"Those were my grandmother's," she said. "We used to use them when I was little and I'd stay with her and watch old movies. She's the one I got a ton of my books from."

"That sounds lovely," I said. My grandparents were all elderly when I was young and died one by one, my last grandfather gone before I turned 13.

"She was," she said, sighing. "I miss her."

Once I was done with setting up the living room to eat, I didn't have anything else to do but watch Tenley zoom around her kitchen, doing fifty things at once.

The chicken came out of the oven and it smelled so good, I was tempted to snatch a piece even if it burned my fingers and made Tenley mad.

She finished up the salad with fresh herbs and I helped her bring everything to the living room, setting the food on a third tray.

"This is really nice, thank you," I said, laying an embroidered napkin on my lap. I didn't even know embroidered napkins were a thing.

"I cook when I'm stressed," Tenley said, filling a bowl full of pasta salad.

"I eat when I'm stressed," I said. She snorted.

The food was absolutely incredible, and I couldn't stop shoveling more of the pasta salad into my mouth. Tenley had put on a playlist, which was good because I couldn't pause eating long enough to say much.

A heavy sigh from Tenley interrupted me.

"Sorry," she said when I looked over at her.

"No worries," I said, quickly swallowing so I didn't speak with food in my mouth. "It's been a shitty weekend."

"That it has," she said. "Fuck, I can't believe I have a deadline." She rubbed her forehead, as if she was getting a headache.

"A writing deadline?" I was endlessly curious about her writing career.

"Yeah. It's been a little hard to write lately with everything happening with Shane. Not only has he fucked with my heart, but he's fucking with my career." She stabbed her fork into an olive and glared at it, as if the olive was the one who wronged her.

"Is there any way to ask for an extension?" I asked.

Tenley shook her head. "No. I have to stick to my release schedule. It's too complicated to explain, but there's no getting around it. I've written through worse, but all I want to do is lay in bed and cry for a week. And eat as many varieties of cheese as I can find in this forsaken town."

I let out a bark of laughter at the image of Tenley lying in bed, surrounded by cheese.

"Sorry. We can go get you some cheese, if you want," I said.

"I'll be fine," she said. "I always am."

"Why do you go write at Common Grounds every day? Not that I don't love having you there to bother me," I said, bumping her shoulder with mine.

"If I didn't leave my house, I would never get anything done.

When the choice is doing work or reading, I'm almost always going to choose reading. Obviously." She waved at her shelves and piles and stacks. "I love writing, don't get me wrong, but when something is your job, it can be less enticing than reading."

That made sense. I was lucky that when I made my toys, I could put on an audiobook if I wanted because it wouldn't distract me. If only I could do that at my barista job.

"How many books have you published?" I asked.

She thought for a moment. "Twenty? I think?"

I almost choked on a bite of chicken. "Twenty?! That's a fuck ton of books, Tenley, holy shit. How fast do you write?"

She wiggled her fingers. "I type very fast."

How did she come up with that many ideas, though? Her mind was starting to terrify me.

"People liked my fanfic, so I figured why not write and get paid in more than kudos and likes," she said. "And I didn't want to do anything else. I think I'm pretty unemployable at this point."

"Hey, if you're making money at it, then there's no reason to look for something else," I said.

"Do you like being a barista?" she asked. There were a lot of people who made jokes about my job, or were snotty about it, but Tenley's tone was pure curiosity.

"I do. I mean, it has its moments of me wanting to rip my hair out and walk into the sea, but I'm sure writing is like that too. Customers can be a bit much, but I do like it for now. It's not a forever job, since I don't want to move up and be a manager or anything, but it's fine until I decide if I want to do something else."

"I don't know how you do it," Tenley said, wiping her face with her napkin and setting it on the empty plate. "Someone would be an asshole to me, and I'd tell them to fuck off and then I'd be fired."

"I've wanted to tell you to fuck off a few times," I said, glaring at her.

Tenley laughed. "Yeah, I bet you have. But you never said it to my face."

"No. Because I enjoy paying my bills," I said.

Tenley was quiet for a moment.

"I wasn't *that* much of an asshole, was I?"

I smiled. "No. I knew if I really asked you to knock it off, you would. I mean, you were there every day and if I threatened to ban you, your behavior would have changed pretty quick."

Tenley laughed. "Yeah, you're right. Then I'd have to find a new place to go and they wouldn't make macchiatos like you."

"I promise you, I don't do anything special with your macchiatos. They're the same as everyone else's," I said. My stomach simply couldn't fit in any more chicken and pasta salad, so I set my fork down on my plate and sat back on the couch.

"Your macchiatos always taste better than the ones I make," she said, curling her feet up on the couch and pushing her tray away.

"Food and drinks always taste better when you're not the one making them," I said. "I'm sure there's some study somewhere about it."

Tenley leaned her head against a pillow. "Fuck, I'm tired again. Breakups are exhausting."

I stood up and grabbed both our plates to take to the kitchen.

"I've got this part," I said when Tenley tried to stop me. The least I could do was throw a few things in the dishwasher for her.

Once the trays were put away, Tenley had gotten cozy on the couch with a crocheted blanket draped on her lower half.

"My grandmother made this," she said, fingering the yarn. "Every year I make a resolution that I'm going to learn to crochet like this and make another one and every year I get distracted by other things."

"I do that too," I said. "I bought watercolor paints years ago and keep forgetting to get them out and use them."

"I can't seem to let myself have a hobby that doesn't make me money," she said through a light laugh. "If I could monetize my reading, I absolutely would."

"That sounds like the ideal job," I said, and we lapsed into silence, but it wasn't uncomfortable.

"You know, you're different than you were in high school," she said, looking at me sideways.

I mirrored her position. "Am I? I don't feel that different. You're definitely the same."

Tenley let out an offended noise. "I am not! I'm completely different than I was in high school."

"Tenley. You were dating the same guy and hanging out with the exact same people until five minutes ago," I said.

She opened her mouth to argue with me and then snapped it closed.

"Well, I'm not with Shane anymore, and I'm probably not going to be friends with them anymore. I'm on my own," she said, but she didn't sound happy. "They're all going to pick Shane."

"Not necessarily," I said. "Some of them might surprise you."

"Shut up, you hate them," Tenley said.

"I don't hate them," I said.

"Liar," she said, pointing at me. "You're such a liar."

"Karissa seems cool," I said.

"She is. We've had our issues in the past, but when she found out we were 'dating,' she was really nice about it," she said.

"Yeah, what are you going to do about that?" I asked.

"What am I going to do about what?" she asked, but she absolutely knew what I was talking about.

"Everyone thinks your queer now, Tenley. Are you going to tell them that you're not?" I asked.

"Are *you*?" she shot back at me, sitting up straight.

"They're not my friends. I don't care what they think about me," I said. That was the truth. Now that I wasn't trapped with them in high school, they didn't have any power over me.

"No, I'm not going to tell them because then I'll be the girl who faked being gay and that's so much worse than them thinking I'm gay. Besides, bisexuality exists."

"And pansexuality," I pointed out. Sydney and Honor were both pansexual.

"Exactly. Just because I dated a woman once, doesn't mean I can't date guys going forward," she said, her chin jutting out.

"You don't have to convince me," I said, putting my hands up. "I'm not attacking you."

"It feels like you are," she said, pouting.

"I'm not, promise," I said.

Tenley huffed and picked up the remote. "Want to watch something?" Her quick pivot made me pause, but I wasn't here to harass her while she was down. So I shut my mouth and didn't say anything else as she flipped through her apps in search of something to watch.

∽

TENLEY SETTLED on the same reality show we'd been watching together what felt like a thousand years ago, but was really earlier today.

"Do you want ice cream?" she asked me a little while later.

"Always," I said. There was no situation in which I'd say no to ice cream.

Tenley hopped up and went to the freezer. She came back holding two pints in her hands.

"This one or this one?" she asked me, holding them out so I could read the labels.

"That one," I said, selecting the strawberry cheesecake pint.

"Sprinkles?" she asked.

"Yes, please," I called. I'd paused the show while Tenley got the ice cream ready. I would have just eaten it out of the container, but she put it in fancy cut-glass bowls that I assumed must also be from her grandmother.

"Thanks," I said, taking it from her. Tenley had a bowl full of brownie batter with a moderate amount of sprinkles. She'd given me tons.

"How do you join the book club at Mainely Books?" she asked when I restarted the show.

"You can just come," I said. "I'll give you the email address and you can get on the newsletter and email chain. The next meeting is on Thursday, but you can still come and just hang out. No one has to speak or even read the book. There have been people who didn't read the books and just come for the food and the gossip and sit and knit or scroll their phones the whole time. We take all kinds," I said.

Tenley scooped up a big chunk of brownie from her ice cream and devoured it.

"That sounds pretty chill," she said.

"Yeah, it is. A book club for people who aren't into joining a book club. The bookstore also has a liquor license, so there's almost always champagne or some fun drink," I said.

"Boozy book club? Why didn't you say so in the first place? I would have joined a long time ago."

I grabbed my phone and sent her the most recent book club newsletter.

"Oh, I've read that already," she said when she opened it. "Can you do me one favor, though?"

"What is it?" I asked.

Tenley set her phone down and looked into her ice cream bowl. "Can you not tell anyone at book club that I'm an author? I like to keep it private."

I nodded. "Yeah, sure."

"Thank you," she said. "I'm not ashamed of it or anything. I just don't like having to answer the same questions over and over." She said it all in a rush.

"It's okay, Tenley. Your secret is safe with me."

"Thanks," she said, going for another brownie chunk. "Someday I want to do book signings and appearances, but I'm not ready yet."

I could picture Tenley, sitting behind a table with a line of people breathlessly holding books and waiting for her to give them a moment of her time and a signature inside their book.

"Do you ever mess up and use your real name?" I asked.

"No, it's pretty easy to keep those two parts of my brain separate. Most of the time. It's fun to be someone else," she said.

"That sounds awesome. I'd love to be someone else sometimes," I said.

"If only I could just be my author alter ego and abandon all my responsibilities," she said. "I'd live like one of those real old-school romance writers with lots of caftans and assistants to cater to my every whim and a fantastic and opulent vacation home. No one would dare upset me."

Tenley sighed.

Something warm spread in my chest at Tenley sharing these desires with me. Like I was getting let in on more of her secrets. I collected them all and held them close, each one like a little treasure.

"Sometimes I wish I could win the lottery and let myself

get really weird. It wouldn't matter if people thought I was weird because I'd be rich and their opinions wouldn't matter. I'd get a bunch of strange pets and paint my house bright colors and grow hundreds of heirloom tomatoes and go on yoga retreats," I said.

Tenley nodded. "I like the way your mind works, Mia."

"Same," I said, and we clinked our spoons together.

∼

YET AGAIN, there was no reason for me to still be at Tenley's house, but here I was, watching silly reality shows and eating tons of ice cream and talking about everything and nothing.

There was an ease to being with Tenley that I couldn't put my finger on. As much as I'd felt judged by her in high school, I didn't anymore. Somehow. When had that changed?

My comfort with Tenley was very…uncomfortable. Not something I wanted to analyze or put too much thought into.

"You know, if you need me to put in a good word for you with a guy, I can vouch for your kissing skills," she said after our second round of ice cream.

What made her say that?

"Thanks, I think?" I said.

"It's true," she said, staring at the TV. "You are a good kisser."

Would it be weird to tell her that she was also a good kisser? That she was the best kisser I'd ever encountered in my life? No, her ego didn't need any more boosting.

"Have you ever kissed another woman? I never asked you," Tenley said. Well, shit.

"Once or twice," I said. That wasn't a total lie. It was just a lot more than twice.

Tenley leaned toward me a little. "Tell me." Her golden eyes were intent on my face, as if she was hanging on my every word. I shifted, uncomfortable with this level of focus from her.

I guess this was it. I could no longer lie to her.

"I'm a lesbian," I said, closing my eyes so I couldn't see her reaction.

When she didn't make a sound, I squinted my eyes open. Tenley stared at me with her mouth open. As if this new information had completely stunned her immoble.

"I'm sorry I lied to you," I said when she still didn't react. Tenley closed her mouth, opened it again, made a sound and then stood up from the couch.

"You're a lesbian," she said, and it wasn't a question.

"Yeah," I said.

"For how long?"

"My whole life?" I said.

She closed her eyes for a second. "How long have you *known?*"

"Oh, I mean, I always knew, but I came out in college." Tenley started pacing in front of the couch.

"Did you know in high school?" she asked.

"I did. I just didn't want to come out. I wasn't ready," I said. "I really am sorry. I kept wanting to tell you and then I figured it didn't matter because we were done."

Tenley abruptly faced me, pointing an accusing finger. "You lied to me."

"I mean, yeah, but it's not like I'm required to disclose my sexuality to anyone and everyone," I said, starting to get annoyed. I owed *no one* my sexuality.

Tenley shook her head and started pacing again. "I would never, ever have asked you to do this if I knew that, Mia. Why did you agree to it?"

"I've been asking myself that same fucking question this entire time. I don't know. You just looked so devastated that day when you came in and then it was so easy to say yes to you.

I mean, I did get a lobster dinner out of it," I said, trying to lighten the mood. Tenley crossed her arms and then sat on the couch again.

"Okay, I have to admit that I'm a little mad that you lied to me. I can't help that. But I have to ask you something and I'm going to need you to be honest when you answer."

I licked my suddenly dry lips. There was a pit in my stomach and I absolutely knew what she was going to ask before the words left her lips.

"Did you agree to fake date me because you're into me?" she asked carefully.

Fuck.

Chapter Ten

"No!" I immediately yelled. "No. No! I promise I didn't." Not at the time, definitely not.

Tenley's eyes narrowed as she studied me, and I tried not to flinch or blush or give any indication that I might have other-than-platonic feelings toward her.

"So you didn't agree to be my fake girlfriend in hopes of being my real girlfriend?" she asked, as if she wanted to be absolutely sure.

"No, I didn't. Besides, you're not even queer, so it wouldn't matter if I was into you anyway." Falling for a straight girl was a right of passage that I had left behind long ago. I was beyond that point in my life.

"Right," she said, as if just remembering that she was straight. "I wouldn't date you anyway. Even if I was into women."

"Ouch," I said, putting my hand over my chest. "I wouldn't date you either. I can do sooooo much better."

I breathed a sigh of relief that we were back to teasing and picking at each other.

Tenley raised one eyebrow. "There's no one better than me. I'd ruin you for everyone else."

I tried to laugh, but I choked on a breath and started coughing.

"Do you need some water?" Tenley asked, and I shook my head.

"I'm good," I said when I could breathe normally again.

"I'm not saying she's near as fantastic as I am, but Karissa is single," she said. "I could put in a good word for you. If she's your type."

That thought had crossed my mind ever since Karissa had said she was pansexual, but I just…I didn't see it. When I thought about her, there was no flutter in my chest, no warmth. None of that instant feeling when you felt something for someone else. The spark just wasn't there. Not to say that it couldn't develop, but for right now, I wasn't feeling it.

"No, thanks. My friends are already on the lookout for me," I said with a laugh.

"There are a lot of queer people in Arrowbridge, I've noticed," Tenley said.

"It's true. This whole area has had an influx for some reason," I said. "Very different than when we were growing up."

"Is that why you didn't want to come out in high school?" she asked. "There were more than a few I remember."

"I know," I said, feeling uncomfy with this particular topic.

"Sorry," Tenley said. "You don't have to defend yourself to me."

We were both silent for a few moments, each lost in thought.

"I should probably get going," I said, even though the prospect of going back to my empty apartment made me want to curl up into a ball. I really should look into getting a pet of some sort. Even fish would be something living and breathing to talk to, even if they didn't answer back.

"You haven't overstayed your welcome, if that's what you're thinking. I mean, you could stay over if you want. I have plenty of bedrooms I'm not using," Tenley said, gesturing to the upstairs. I hadn't been up there, but I had assumed that with the size of the house, there were at least two or more bedrooms.

"Originally I thought I was going to have roommates in this house but then I remembered that I despise most people so now I just have a guest room, an office, and one bedroom that serves as my closet and makeup room. even though I still do my makeup every day while sitting on the floor in front of the mirror in my bedroom," she said.

"Living with strangers in college was more than enough for me," I said. "It's one of the reasons I waited so long to get my own place. I wanted to be able to afford it without someone else."

"Not even Lark? You two are pretty close," she said.

"Exactly. I wouldn't want living with her to completely destroy our friendship," I said, laughing. "Besides, she's very happy with Sydney and I wouldn't want to be around all of that *all* the time."

"They seem pretty good together, from what I've seen," Tenley said.

"You'll get a full dose of it on Thursday at book club. There are so many couples going now, it's kind of ridiculous," I said.

"Mmm, just what I need. Happy couples," Tenley said, frowning.

I reached out and squeezed her hand. "It won't always hurt like this."

Tenley's eyes filled up with tears and she gave me a sad

smile. "I'm going to be really excited to get to the anger part of the grief process."

"Call me when that happens. I'll help you burn all his shit," I said, standing up and going to get my shoes.

"I knew I put in that fire pit in the backyard for a reason," she said, following me with slumped shoulders.

"Hey," Tenley said when I stood up from putting my shoes on. "I know you didn't have to come over and I owe you about 500 favors, but thank you for coming over. I know you're not my fake girlfriend anymore, but we could still…you know. Hang out. I have a lot of free time now." Her laugh was more sad than anything.

"We can hang out," I said. "You can start by repaying the favors by letting me borrow books from your library." Having Tenley's books as a source of reading material was going to save me a lot of money. Arrowbridge did have a library, but it was pretty small and lacking especially in enough sapphic romances.

Tenley pressed her lips together and I could tell she was fighting with herself about letting me borrow books.

"I didn't ruin that last book," I said. "And I gave you a bookmark."

Tenley inhaled through her nose. "You did. It was in good condition when you gave it back. I think we can come to some kind of arrangement."

"Great," I said, and leaned forward to give her a hug on an impulse. Tenley froze for a second, as if she wasn't sure what she was supposed to do. I held her until her arms went around me and I felt her relax into me. Her breath stirred my hair and I felt her heart pounding in her chest.

"Thanks for being my fake girlfriend," she said in a soft voice.

"You're welcome, Tenley," I said. "It was a pleasure."

I walked out the front door and didn't look back, no matter how much I wanted to.

∼

"GOOD MORNING," Tenley said when she arrived at the coffee shop the next morning to work. She looked a whole lot better than she had when I'd seen her last. Her eyes were brighter, and she didn't look like she'd spent hours crying.

"I brought you something," she said, pushing a paperback across the counter toward me. I looked at the cover and the author's name rang a bell.

"Lexi Starr. Isn't she the one you asked me about?" I asked.

"This is an advanced copy I got for her next book. She's a friend, so she sent it to me. Obviously it's not completely edited, so if you see any typos, please ignore them," she said.

"Wow, thanks. I've never read a book before it came out before," I said. I wanted to read the blurb on the back, but I had to actually do my job.

"What can I get for you?" I asked, setting the book aside on a shelf.

"Croissant and an iced honey lavender macchiato. Large. Very large. I have a ton of work that I'm behind on," she said. I punched in the order.

"You got it," I said.

"Thanks, fake ex-girlfriend," she said, skipping off to her table. I shook my head and tried not to smile too much.

∼

"OKAY, you have to let me read this, it sounds hot as fuck," Lark said in a low voice as she checked out the book that Tenley had lent me.

"Yeah, it sounds seriously sexy. I looked up the author on

my break and it's fully erotic romance," I said. I'd also read an excerpt from one of the author's other series and I'd been blushing ever since. Hot AF.

"Damn," Lark said, fanning herself with the book.

"Give me that," I said, taking it from her. "Tenley will murder me if I let anything happen to this." I headed to the back and put the book in my bag so it didn't get coffee or anything else spilled all over it.

When I came back out, Lark was taking Karissa's order.

"Hey," she said to me as I worked on some dishes in the sink. If there was one thing I could change about my job, other than some of the entitled customers, it was the amount of dishes I had to do in a given day.

"Hey," I said back to her. "How's it going?"

"Oh, you know, work," she said, gesturing to her business casual outfit that she wore as a bank teller.

"Same," I said, laughing.

"Hopefully yours has been better than mine. We had to ask a guy to leave because we can't stop the government from garnishing his wages for back child support he owes. I don't know why he expected to find sympathy from us," she said, shaking her head.

"Some people have a lot of audacity," I said, which was a much more polite thing than what I wanted to say.

Karissa smiled. "I know exactly what you mean."

Lark finished her drink and handed it over to her. "Thanks so much. I'll see you around?"

"Yeah, sure," I said. "Hope the rest of your day is better."

Karissa rolled her eyes. "Here's hoping."

She left and I watched her cross the parking lot and head back into the bank.

"Well," Lark said, leaning on the counter and looking at me. "She's cute."

"I guess," I said. Karissa absolutely was cute, but that wasn't what Lark was implying.

"You know she was flirting with you, right?" Lark said, taking a sip of water.

I scoffed. "She wasn't flirting with me. She was making small talk."

"She was absolutely flirting," Lark said. "Do you not want her to flirt with you?"

"I mean...are you asking if I'm into her?" I asked. Lark nodded.

"No," I said. "I'm not into her. She's pretty and seems fun, but it's just not there."

Lark nodded. "I get it. You either feel the spark or you don't. It's too bad, though. She works right across the street and you'd be cute together, but if you're not feeling it than there's nothing to say. I'll still be on the lookout."

I was grateful that Lark dropped the Karissa thing so quickly. She was right that falling for Karissa would be logical, but when had hearts ever been logical?

∼

TENLEY WAS WAITING for me by my car when I left.

"Stalker," I said.

"Not stalking. Just wondering if you were doing anything for dinner? I'll cook."

I'd been planning on going over to Lark and Sydney's for dinner tonight, so I didn't have to cook anyway, but the pull of Tenley's company and her library was just a little bit stronger.

"Can I go home and shower first?" I asked.

"Sure, but I have to admit, I don't mind the smell of espresso," she said. As far as service jobs went, smelling like coffee and chocolate all the time wasn't the worst. Even after I showered, I swore that my hair still retained the smell, but I'd had no complaints.

"Give me an hour?" I asked. That would give me enough time to shower and dry my hair and get cute and decompress from the day.

"Yeah, just come over whenever. I'm making salmon and panzanella." My mouth instantly started watering. "I'll see you in about an hour."

"Should I bring anything?" I asked as Tenley headed toward her car.

"Just yourself," she called back as she unlocked her driver's side.

That I could do.

∽

WHILE I DIDN'T WANT to look like I'd tried too hard with my outfit, I didn't just throw on anything when I got out of the shower. I had a new cute dress I'd been saving for a night out, but this seemed like the right time to wear it.

I put it on and dried my hair before doing a loose braid that made me feel like I escaped from the fey realm. The dress had puffed sleeves that also helped with the look.

Music greeted me when I walked into Tenley's house, and I could hear her singing along from the kitchen. Even though she'd told me I didn't have to bring anything, I had some French chocolates that my parents had sent that I knew she was going to like, and I didn't want to eat all of them by myself. Some treats were better when they were shared.

"Hey," I said, raising my voice as I joined her in the kitchen and set the box of chocolates down on her granite countertop. She turned the music down and beamed at me. She had changed too, but into a pastel sports bra and shorts set with a thin button up on top. There was a whole lot of skin to look at, and I forgot how to speak for a few moments.

"Hey, you're just in time. The salmon is coming out in five minutes," she said, throwing some tomatoes into the salad bowl. "You look gorgeous, are you going somewhere after this?"

I snorted. "Where is there to go in Arrowbridge after nine p.m.?"

Tenley laughed. "Why do you think we're always hanging out in Tommy's barn? Nothing else is open that late."

She dusted off her hands and then plucked a piece of cheese from the salad and popped it into her mouth.

"I brought you a little something," I said, sliding the box toward her. Tenley's eyes lit up.

"What do we have here?" she asked, undoing the ribbon on the box and opening it up.

"My parents periodically send me boxes of French sweets, so I decided to share some with you," I said.

"I'm sorry, I didn't hear anything you said over the sound of chocolate," she said, wiggling her fingers as she tried to select a chocolate.

I chuckled and then watched as Tenley finally picked one and took a bite, her eyes rolling back on her head as she let out a soft moan.

Fucckkkkkkk. I hadn't known she was going to do that. Between the moaning and the outfit, I was starting to get warm in the kitchen.

"You are officially my favorite person," she said once she'd finished the chocolate and licked her fingers.

"You're welcome," I said, my voice rough as I cleared my throat.

I was saved by the timer going off so Tenley had to take the salmon out of the oven. She set it on a metal rack to cool a little bit before serving. It smelled absolutely heavenly.

This time I knew where the plates were, so I pulled them out and set up the trays and it was a little unnerving how comfortable I was in her house. Tenley's house was just so cozy that it was hard not to relax here. The books and the cozy furniture and bright colors just soothed me. I had even seen a few things that inspired me to make some updates in my own apartment.

Tenley set up the salmon and salad and also brought in a bottle of crisp white wine.

"Cheers, doll," Tenley said, and my stomach did a little micro-flip at her calling me "doll." So much different than when we'd been in public calling each other "babe" so people would think we were together.

"Cheers," I said before almost inhaling a sip of wine right into my lungs.

The salmon was so good that I briefly considered licking my plate. The panzanella salad was totally delicious and full of fresh tomatoes and still-crusty sourdough bread and olive oil.

Without even asking, Tenley put on the show we'd been watching together and started the next episode. Like we did this every night. Watching this show had become our thing. Our routine.

I gulped some wine so I didn't think about that too much. There was no law that said I couldn't be friends with Tenley now that I wasn't pretending to be her girlfriend. I could be her friend while remembering exactly how she kissed. How she tasted. How relentless her tongue was. People had done it before.

"A few of my friends have reached out," Tenley said after a lull in our conversation.

"Is that a good thing?" I asked.

"I mean, it was all pretty much that they're sorry that we broke up and to reach out if I need anything, but it's clear that they're choosing Shane over me. Just what I thought would happen." She sighed and gave me a tight smile.

"That blows," I said.

"It does. Karissa was the only one who said something nice and asked me if I wanted to hang out with her," she said. I'd seen Karissa go over to Tenley at the coffee shop today and had wondered what Karissa had said.

"Are you going to?" I asked.

"I think so. Like I said, she and I have never been close, but maybe it's time we change that. I do love her hair," she said.

"She does have great hair."

Tenley pulled some of her hair in front of her face. "I want to do something with my hair. It's so boring."

"Your hair is not boring," I said. Tenley's color was gorgeous, like honey when hit with sunlight, and since I'd never seen her with roots, I was pretty sure it was natural.

"Easy for you to say, princess ginger," she said.

"Princess ginger?" I said, almost choking. "That's a new one." I'd been called all kinds of things for having red hair and most of them weren't that complimentary.

"Your hair is gorgeous, do you know how many people would love to have that color?" Tenley said.

"Yeah, I could say the same about you, blondie."

Tenley made a face. "I still think I could do something cool."

"My friend Everly has pink hair," I said. "But she has to bleach the hell out of it to get it that way and constantly touch up the color."

Tenley waved that off. "Way too much work. But I could do a color streak or something." She pulled some more hair in front of her face and thought about it.

"Or maybe I'll chop it off," she said, studying the ends of her hair.

"Do whatever you want. It grows back," I said, picturing Tenley with different haircuts.

"I've never had short hair in my life," she said. "My mom would never let me cut it because she said it would make me look like a boy, so I just never did."

"Ugh, that's so annoying. I hate it when parents do shit like that." I was glad my parents never had, but only because they hadn't cared enough about my appearance. I could have shaved my entire head and they probably would have just shrugged.

"You could always start with cutting a few inches and go from there."

"Hmm," Tenley said, and I could tell she was lost in thought about her hair.

"Shane always told me that he didn't like short hair," she said. Typical. Some men were so fucking fragile.

"Sorry, I just keep thinking about all the things I didn't do because he didn't like them," she said, giving me an apologetic smile.

"That sounds really shitty," I said. First her parents and then her boyfriend? Tenley had been stifled for a long time.

"It didn't feel like that at the time. It felt like a compliment somehow. Now I know it wasn't." She made a face and then let out a frustrated sound.

"Oh my god, I just realized I'm never going to have sex again," she said, rubbing her face.

I definitely didn't want to talk about this, so I didn't comment.

"Not that what I had with Shane was mind-blowing by any means. We'd been together for a long time, if you know what I mean." It seemed that Tenley had gotten on a tangent again and nothing was going to slow her down and I'd have to hold on for dear life.

"I don't," I said, wishing my wine glass wasn't empty. The bottle was too far away for me to reach.

"Let's just say that things can get stale, and if your partner is happy with the way things are, then you're kind of fucked. And not in a good way." How much wine had Tenley had?

"Uhhh," I said, searching around for a way, any way, to change the current topic.

Tenley grabbed the bottle of wine and filled up her glass. I managed to snatch the bottle from her. I was going to need it, so I filled my glass with what was left.

"Shane was going to propose this year," she said, which was better than talking about her sex life, but not by much. "At least he told me he was. He wanted to buy a house too."

I remembered she'd been fighting with him on the phone about houses. I thought it was kind of interesting that they didn't live together, even after being together for so long.

Tenley blew out a breath. "It doesn't matter now. None of that shit matters now. At least I don't have to get a divorce or find a new place to live."

"Seriously," I said, and Tenley drained her glass of wine, setting it down on her tray with a frown.

"I'm doing that thing where I only talk about myself again. I promise I'm not normally this self-centered. I mean, I am self-centered, but I can hold a decent conversation like an adult," she said.

I knew how to get her to talk about something else.

"What are you reading right now?" I asked and watched as her face completely changed, like the sun coming out from behind the clouds.

∽

AGAIN, I stayed way too late at Tenley's house.

"See you tomorrow," she said, hugging me. This time I was the one who was surprised.

"Your hair still smells like coffee," she said in my ear and a shiver went down my spine.

Her hair smelled like…some flower I couldn't put my finger on. Probably something fancy and expensive.

Tenley leaned into me, letting out a little "mmm" sound that made a bolt of heat go through my body. I'd never gotten horny from a hug before, so this was a first.

This friendship thing wasn't really working out if I was getting turned on by a very tame hug.

I had a serious problem.

Chapter Eleven

TENLEY ASKED me if I wanted to come over for dinner on Tuesday and Wednesday, but I told her I already had plans. What I needed right now was some distance; I felt like I'd been spending all my time with her and I needed space to get my head together. It was hard to think when she was right there, looking all gorgeous and calling me "doll."

Instead, I went over to Ingrid's on Tuesday after picking Athena up at daycare, and went over to Lark and Sydney's on Wednesday. They were full of questions about what was happening with Tenley.

"She's coming to book club," I said. "And don't ask her about the whole fake relationship thing. She doesn't know that you two know and I'd like to keep it that way."

Tenley would probably be pissed about that, but she couldn't expect me to keep that whole thing a secret from my best friend and her girlfriend.

"We promise not to grill her too much," Lark said.

"Speak for yourself, I'm absolutely going to grill her," Sydney said. "I want to know all the details about her breakup."

I gave Sydney a look. "She's still really devastated. I know Shane is the actual worst, but she really did love him."

Sydney made a disgusted face. "I guess you really can't choose who you love."

"You should know. You tried so hard not to love me. Do you not remember the denial?" Lark said, snorting with laughter.

"Mmm, that was some sweet denial," Sydney said, puckering her lips for a kiss. "I got there in the end, didn't I?"

"Eventually," Lark said, tapping Sydney on the nose. They stayed lost in each other for a moment before remembering that I was there. Sometimes I had even waved to remind them they weren't alone. They were so cute I didn't mind. Mostly.

"Don't worry, we'll be nice to Tenley. I feel like I know a completely different person from what you've told us about her," Sydney said.

"She's not an easy person to get to know," I said. It wasn't until she opened up about how much she loved books that I really saw the person behind the girl I'd known in high school. That perfect, popular girl who was always laughing, always having a good time, always had the sun shining on her. I guess I'd never truly seen her as a whole person, with problems and dreams and passions just like everyone else.

That realization rocked me a little. So many of the assumptions I'd made about Tenley were so off base. I'd wanted to think those things about her because it made her a lot easier to dislike. Sure, she'd given me a few reasons to dislike her, but she hadn't earned all the ire I'd been holding onto and building up over the years.

It was time to grow the fuck up and leave that high school shit behind. Didn't mean I was going to give Shane a free pass, because that man was still a giant fucking cold sore. Didn't mean I was going to the next barn party. But I could at least let go of all that shit with Tenley. Just let it *go*.

"Mia?" Lark said, and I realized I'd been totally checked out while I had my little epiphany.

"Yeah, sorry. Just checked out for a second," I said, feeling my face go red.

"You looked like you were thinking about something real hard there," Sydney said.

"I'm good," I said, getting up from my chair. "Anyone want anything while I'm up?"

"Can you grab my other bottle of hot sauce? It's on the counter," Sydney said, shaking the near empty bottle she had.

"You got it," I said, grabbing another one of the cookies that Lark had made, as well as the hot sauce for Sydney, mentally pushing my revelations about Tenley aside. For now.

∼

"I GUESS I'll see you in a little bit," Tenley said after she'd packed up her work for the day at Common Grounds. She was leaving earlier than she usually did, probably to shower and change before book club. Not that there was any kind of dress code. Sometimes Joy would have us do a color theme, or we'd wear something that was mentioned in a book, but not for this meeting.

"See you later," I said, wiping down the pick-up counter. Tenley wiggled her fingers at me and walked out the door and I turned around to find Lark smirking at me.

"What?" I asked, scrubbing the same spot on the counter so I didn't have to keep looking at her face.

"You might not be fake dating her anymore, but you haven't stopped looking at her like that," she said. I glanced up from the counter.

"Like what?" I asked, knowing exactly how I'd been looking at Tenley. I'd just been hoping no one else had noticed.

Lark looked around and then stepped close to me. "Like

you want to—" She stuck her tongue between two fingers held up in a V and laughed.

"Jesus *Christ*, Lark," I said, going twelve different shades of red. "It's a good thing Liam didn't walk out here and find you doing that."

She cackled and gently shoved me. "You should have seen the look on your face."

"You know, I think Sydney is rubbing off on you," I said. That motion was something she definitely would have done.

"Mmm, she definitely is," Lark said, raising and lowering her eyebrows.

"Gross, Lark," I said, making a face. She just laughed and I couldn't help but be happy for her. She adored Sydney and was adored in return.

I wanted that. I wanted it so much.

I went back to cleaning to try and stop myself from thinking about it.

∾

LARK AND I both tried to rush out of work so we'd have enough time to get home and get cute for book club. The previous night I'd set out my planned outfit, so all I had to do when I got home was take a quick shower, do something with my hair, and get dressed before walking down the stairs and then around the building so I could enter Mainely Books from the front.

"Whoa," I said when I walked in. Since the book we read took place in a café, Joy had gotten lots of cute café decorations, as well as pink balloons and streamers.

She and Ezra were still running around and setting everything up, so at least I wasn't late.

"Hey, good to see you," Joy said, giving me a bright smile and a quick hug.

"It looks beautiful, as always," I said.

"Thank you," Joy said, beaming from the praise. She put her heart and soul into every single meeting of this club, and I didn't think she'd ever know how much it meant to everyone that she did. Book club wasn't just about the reading. It was a safe space where sometimes, we had put aside the books and let people just vent about their shit in a safe space. We had come together more than once to raise money for members, or to support someone when they were going through something. It really was a community, and I was so grateful for it.

"I know it's late, so caffeine can be tricky, so we have a lot of decaf on hand," Joy said. "But coffee is probably the last thing you want to drink right now."

"You'd be right about that," I said. Although, I did love an espresso martini every now and then.

"Well help yourself and get a chair and we'll start when everyone gets here," Joy said, fiddling with the arrangement of cupcakes on the table. Layne had been here already, because there was a plate of incredible-looking brownies, and I didn't miss the trio of dips nestled with various crudité and chips. Drawn more to the voices in the back of the shop than the food, I headed around the shelves to the little area where members were setting the chairs in a circle.

Lark, Sydney, Layne, Honor, Everly, and Ryan were already here, along with a number of other people. So many of us tried to get here early to ease the burden on Joy.

"This is all pretty fancy," a voice said behind me and I turned to find Tenley standing behind me wearing a faded bookish t-shirt and jeans.

"Yeah, Joy does an incredible job," I said.

Tenley's eyes flicked to the group that was already gathered and chatting with each other.

"You going to introduce me, or how does this work?" she

asked, standing so close to me I could feel the heat from her skin.

"I can, if you want," I said. "We get people coming in and out, but there's no pressure to stand up and say your name and three facts about yourself or anything like that."

Tenley snorted. "I would, if I had to. I don't mind speaking in public."

No, she definitely did not. I'd forgotten that she'd been in the drama club in high school and had been in several of the school plays.

I led her back toward everyone else and immediately Lark came over.

"Hey, it's weird seeing you outside of CG and without your laptop," Lark said.

"Sometimes it feels like I'm surgically attached to it, I swear," Tenley said. "When you're self-employed, you work all the time."

"Truth," Sydney said. "Hey, it's nice to see you, Tenley."

"Yeah, it's been a while," Tenley said, but she wasn't unfriendly.

Everyone else swarmed over, eager to see a new face, so Tenley got introduced to a lot of people at once, but she smiled and laughed and shook hands and charmed absolutely everyone. Shocker.

At one point, she snagged my arm and said, "I'm absolutely starving, come get food with me?" in my ear.

Tenley reaching for me made my heart thump hard in my chest.

"Let's go get some food," I said and we beelined for the table. I handed her a plate and she piled it high.

"This all looks amazing," she said, scooping dips onto her plate and then adding carrots and chips and cucumber slices. "I didn't have dinner before I came and now my stomach is angry. I get so busy working sometimes I forget to eat. That's one of the reasons I go to the coffee shop. I can stand up and go right for the counter and get something quick so my blood sugar doesn't crash." I hadn't thought of it that way.

"I'm happy to help your blood sugar not crash," I said, putting two brownies on my plate and balancing things out with a few cherry tomatoes and cucumbers.

Someone else had brought little caprese skewers and there were always tons of crackers and an assortment of cheeses. We didn't mess around with the snacks at book club. Even if you haven't read the book, you wouldn't go home hungry or thirsty.

"Drink?" I asked Tenley.

"Absolutely yes," she said, and I handed her a cup of pink wine, and then selected one for myself. She followed me back to the chairs and took the one right next to me. There was quite a crowd here tonight, so Tenley and I were pretty close. Lark took the spot on my other side, but she leaned close to Sydney as they shared their plates.

"Are we ready to get started?" Joy asked as she stood in front of her chair. Ezra sat next to her with the discussion questions on Joy's tablet, and a bottle of water for Joy. While the group was informal, there still was a structure, and each meeting had unique questions and discussion.

"Is there anyone who wanted to introduce themselves?" Joy asked, staring right at Tenley.

"Hi," Tenley said, waving. "I'm Tenley. I think I know quite a few of you already, but this is my first book club meeting ever, so please be gentle with me. I did read the book, so hopefully I'll have something interesting to say."

There were a few chuckles at that, and Tenley shared her beautiful smile. No wonder she was so popular in high school. There was just some sort of extra *something* about her that you couldn't put your finger on, but you knew it when you saw it and then you wanted to be around it.

"Welcome, Tenley," Joy said and then asked for people to

share their first impressions of the book. A few people spoke about the coziness of the story, how much they liked that the protagonist was an older divorced woman who had children. Quite a few members of our club were older moms who had discovered their own bisexuality or pansexuality later in life. Some were still working on it. No one was required to disclose their label to join, obviously, but many had been drawn to the club in ways they couldn't put to words and then realized a few months later exactly why.

Tenley had no qualms about speaking and sharing how much she'd like the setting of the cozy coffeeshop and she said she enjoyed seeing how the protagonist's friends supported her, but she still struggled with coming out, even with a lesbian best friend.

I couldn't take my eyes off her as she spoke. She was magical. Funny and witty and bright. I'd known all this, but it was really on display at book club. She piggybacked off comments others had made and her observations deepened my own understanding and enjoyment of the book.

We took a break to refuel and Tenley joined me in line for more snacks.

"You're starting off strong with book club. Are you sure you haven't done this before?" I asked.

"I mean, I do talk about books with my author friends," she said, leaning in and whispering so no one would hear about her being an author. "I guess this is a little bit like that, but with more structure. I'm enjoying it. Everyone seems so kind."

"They are. And I'm pretty sure everyone adores you already," I said.

Tenley grinned. "Of course they do. I'm adorable."

She certainly was.

EVENTUALLY PEOPLE STARTED DRIFTING out after the conversation had moved from our current book to the suggestions for the next one (which were also sent out via email for anyone who missed the meeting), and then general discussion and the airing of grievances. What was a book club without that?

We officially broke for the night and I always stayed to help put away chairs and pack up leftovers and clean up. The bonus to helping was getting to take home some delicious desserts and dips, which didn't hurt.

Tenley hung around, chatting with anyone and everyone. She wasn't helping, but she wasn't leaving either.

"I feel like I'm buzzed off book club," she said to me as I piled a plate with some of Layne's brownies.

"Are you now?" I said, laughing. She was practically dancing on her toes.

"Yes, it's just so good to be with other people talking about books in person. I don't know," she said, her face going a little red as if she was ashamed of her enthusiasm.

"You're cute," I said, and then I was the one turning red. I couldn't make comments like that.

Tenley let out that sweet little giggle that turned me inside out. "Thank you."

What had I been doing? Right, brownies.

Most everyone else had left, and it was time to go upstairs to my apartment. There was a little bit of a letdown after book club. A lot of times I would hang out with Lark and Sydney so it wasn't such an abrupt change from a group of book nerds to a silent apartment.

Tenley let out a loud sigh. "I don't want to go home yet, but nothing is open. I wish there was a bar we could get a drink at or something."

Her lips formed a pout that was absolutely doing something to me.

"I have wine," I blurted out. "It's free to drink at my place. I mean, free for you. But the wine was on sale." Now I was babbling.

Tenley smiled and grabbed the last brownie from the plate.

"I love that idea."

Chapter Twelve

Nerves hit me with full force as Tenley followed me upstairs to my apartment a few minutes later. I had a plate of treats in my hand as Tenley hummed softly to herself. I thought I recognized the song, but I wasn't completely sure.

I unlocked the door and let Tenley inside, setting the plate of treats on the counter. Tenley went immediately to the fridge for the wine while I got the glasses. Had it really been less than a week since she knocked on my door and asked to come in after Shane dumped her again?

Tenley thanked me and went immediately to the couch. I didn't have to tell her to make herself comfortable, because she already did that on her own.

"Have you started this yet?" she asked, holding up the Lexi Starr book.

"I did," I said.

"And?" she asked as I sat next to her.

"It's very…erotic," I said. There was literally fucking in the first chapter and to say it was hot as hell was an understatement.

"Is it?" she asked and then sipped her wine.

"You haven't read it?" I asked. Why would she give me a book she hadn't read?

"Once or twice," she said. "Other than the erotic aspects, are you liking it?" She twirled her glass in her hand and I worried she might drop it.

"I didn't say that I was upset about the erotic aspects. Just that I was surprised. And the writing is very good. I love a book that's super sexy, but then is really poetically written," I said, feeling like I was still at book club or something.

"So you like it?" Tenley asked, gripping her wine glass for dear life. She really wanted me to like her friend's book.

"Yeah, Tenley, I really like it. I've only just started though."

She exhaled a shaky breath.

"Why do you care so much what I think?" I asked.

"Because..." Tenley said, setting her wine on the coffee table. "Because *I* wrote it."

She looked down at her hands and not at me.

"You *wrote* this?" I asked, holding up the book. There was no picture of the author on the back or in the book. Just a picture of a flower and a vague author bio that didn't give any identifying information.

Tenley nodded. "Yes." Her voice was soft.

"You wrote this?" I asked again, holding the book in front of her.

"Yes! I did, okay. Don't make a big thing about it," she said. The confident girl who called herself adorable was gone and I didn't know who this timid person was.

"Tenley, you wrote a *book*. That's fucking amazing," I said, and she glanced up in surprise.

"Really?" she said.

"Yes, really. You're extremely talented, holy shit," I said, floored by this information.

Tenley's smile was so sweet and so heartbreaking at the

same time and it took my breath away. Fuck. She was so beautiful it hurt to look at her.

Tenley leaned closer to me, her cheeks rosy from the praise and her eyes lit up so much that they glowed.

"You're fucking talented, Tenley Hill," I said, and I didn't know who moved first, but before I realized what was happening, her lips were on mine and her tongue was in my mouth.

Did it really matter how it happened? Not so much. It only mattered that it was happening, *finally*.

Finally, finally, *finally*.

Tenley pulled me into her lap and dug her fingers into my skin hard enough to bruise and still, it wasn't close enough.

I craved more, needed *more*.

There was no time to think about Tenley being straight, or her being my fake ex-girlfriend or that she'd literally just broken up with her boyfriend of like seven years. There was only Tenley and me and our bodies in a heated conversation that I was powerless to stop, even if I wanted to.

I didn't.

Her hands yanked up my dress and I pulled at her jeans and both of us got frustrated.

"Wait," she said, pulling back. Fuck. She had probably come to her senses and was going to tell me to get off her.

"Yeah?" I said, my chest heaving as I looked down at her. Tenley's hair was still pulled back and I really wanted to take it down so I could run my fingers through it. Maybe pull on it a little and see if she liked that. I knew I did.

"We need to approach this logically," she said, and I blinked at her.

"Logically?" There wasn't a whole lot of logic driving any of my actions right now. Logic had been banished from my mind, at least for the time being.

"Yes, either you need to take off your dress first, or I need to take off my shirt first. It's almost impossible to do both things at the same time," she said, and I burst out laughing.

"You are a strange and beautiful creature, Tenley," I said, capturing her lips again.

"I hope that's a compliment," she said, arching one eyebrow.

"It is. It definitely is," I said, and even though I liked talking to her, I cared more about getting her naked. Her tits had occupied my thoughts far more times than I was willing to admit.

But since I was the more experienced one, at least with having sex with women, I chose to take the lead by pulling down the zipper in the corner of my dress and sliding one of the straps down my arm.

Tenley's pupils dilated and that made me feel fucking amazing. There was no question that she wanted me. Wanted this. The sexuality discussion could happen later. Much later.

Right now, my only goal was to get her naked and to get her sitting on my face so I could fuck her senseless with my tongue.

Reluctantly I left her lap to get my dress the rest of the way off. Underneath I wore a simple tan seamless bra and boyshort bottoms. They weren't the sexiest thing in my wardrobe, but that didn't seem to matter to Tenley.

I kicked the dress aside and waited as Tenley visually devoured me from my ears to my neck to my chest to my stomach and all the way down my legs even to my toes.

"You're gorgeous," she breathed. "When did that happen?" Her voice had a dreamy quality, as if she couldn't quite believe this was happening. Well, neither could I.

Even two weeks ago, if you told me that I would be standing in front of Tenley Hill, ready to get her naked and sweaty, I would have said you should probably take fewer edibles.

Here I was, and here she was, and she looked at me as if she wanted to devour me. It was only polite to let her. My parents hadn't taught me much, but they had taught me manners.

"Take of your shirt," I said, getting back onto the couch with her, and pulling at the hem of it. She smirked and put her arms up.

"Oh, so I have to undress both of us?" I asked.

Her face disappeared as I pulled the shirt over her head and then threw it aside.

"You have more practice," she said.

"True," I said, reaching to the back of her head to tenderly pull the elastic from her ponytail. Strands of honey fell all over her shoulders and I couldn't stop staring at her black silky bra. This was even better than I could have imagined.

Unable to help myself, I brushed my fingers along one of the cups and she made a little whimpering noise. Tenley's nipples were hard under the soft fabric.

"Let's get these jeans off you, okay?" I said, surprised by how soft my voice was. I got up so Tenley could stand and remove her jeans, doing a cute little shimmy to reveal lacy black bottoms that made me forget my own name for a second.

Her body was so damn good I wanted to ask her to do a turn for me so I could take in every single inch.

"Come here," I said, snagging her waist and pulling her toward me. Our bodies bumped into each other and she gasped out a little laugh before I captured her mouth again, diving one hand into her hair.

Tenley grabbed me and kissed me as her hips started to push toward mine, reaching and seeking.

"Please," she gasped. "*Please.*"

"What do you want, Tenley?" I asked, pushing her hair back and looking into those golden eyes. "What do you want, babe?" This time the word didn't feel like a lie or a performance.

Tenley clamped onto my shoulder and my waist with her hands.

"I haven't had a fucking orgasm in two years. I need to have a fucking orgasm, Mia," she said, her voice breathless.

I tucked a strand of hair behind her ears. Her entire body shook with need and it was hot and cute at the exact same time.

"Babe, I'm going to make you come at least twice. Don't even worry about it." Not only did I have my tongue and my fingers in my arsenal, but I had my extensive toy collection, some of which I'd engineered myself for maximum pleasure.

"You're in good hands," I said, sliding my fingers into her bottoms and finding her soaking wet. Tenley's entire body jerked as I stroked her. She held onto me for dear life and since I didn't want her legs to give out, I brought my hand to my lips and licked my fingers, making eye contact with her so she knew exactly what I was doing.

"You taste so fucking good, babe," I said. "I can't wait to get you all over my face."

"Now," Tenley said. "Now, please."

She was so eager and I couldn't wait. I couldn't fucking wait.

"Come on, babe," I said, sliding my hand into hers. "All my tools are in the bedroom."

"Tools?" Tenley asked.

I pushed open the door and shoved Tenley toward the bed.

"Get your clothes off," I said as I went to my nightstand and the basket underneath that housed my various lubes and lotions. All of my toys and other items had their own little area. All of the toys I'd made were in a special case that I'd had custom made for myself. My other toys were in a box under my bed, and then the other naughty things that I wasn't going to bring out unless Tenley asked, were in a box in my closet. When it came to sexual accessories, I was willing to try just about anything once. Experimentation was one of the best parts of sex, in my opinion.

I set out a few lubes and pulled out the protective pad I put over my comforter so I didn't ruin the bed with all the fun.

Tenley was pulling her bottoms off as I laid out the pad.

"That's smart," she said. "Shane would never let me put anything down." She winced, realizing she'd mentioned her ex.

"It's okay," I said, taking her hand and kissing the back of it. "You're not going to be thinking about him in a few moments." My mission was to make sure that she didn't even remember his name or that he existed. He was nothing. She was everything.

Tenley scooted until she was stretched out on the pad and she didn't seem to know what to do with her hands. I still had my bra and bottoms on, so I figured she'd be more comfortable if she wasn't the only completely naked one.

I unhooked my bra and slid down my bottoms and climbed up next to her, turning on my side to face her.

"Hey," I said, stroking her stomach. She had her belly pierced with a pink stone, which was so Tenley and so cute, I couldn't stand it.

"I don't know what I'm doing," she said, biting her bottom lip. "I mean, I know I literally write sapphic erotica, but you can learn a lot from other authors and from porn."

"Oh, were you watching porn, Tenley?" I asked, my heart rate spiking and my blood running hot.

She licked her lips. "Yeah, I had to learn somehow. I consider my memberships to certain creators a work expense."

I snorted. "You job sounds pretty great."

She smiled slowly. "It is."

"If there's anything you want to try, don't hesitate to tell me. I'm pretty open about everything. There's not much you could say that would shock me." I mean, there was a first for everything, but I was pretty confident.

"Okay," she said, suddenly shy.

"We can start with a kiss. We don't have to go anywhere beyond that," I said. I hadn't had a partner this inexperienced in a while, so I had to recalibrate and go super slow. This had to be good for her, after so many years of terrible sex. She deserved all the orgasms she could handle. And then a few more.

"A kiss sounds good," she said, reaching for me. Our lips met softly for about half a second and then somehow, I ended up on top of her as Tenley thrust her body against mine, seeking friction and pressure. So much for slow.

As much as I wanted to tease her pretty nipples, she needed to come, and she needed to come right now. Once we got the first out of the way, we could take our time and I could tease the next one out of her. And then make her beg for the third. Fuck, I couldn't wait to see her beg. I got wet just picturing it.

I maneuvered myself so I could grind myself against her thigh while I stroked her, getting my fingers completely wet. Guess we didn't need the lube yet.

Every time I brushed her clit, Tenley's body jerked, and I could feel the tremors through her whole body. She was so wound up that I knew it wouldn't take much, so I started rubbing circles on her clit, not even bothering to fuck her inside.

"Yes, yes, yes," Tenley panted, her eyes shuttering closed. I added more speed and pressure and watched as she shattered under me, just a few seconds before I came myself, shuddering above her and gasping out her name. That first orgasm was quick and hard and just a teaser of things to come.

I rolled next to Tenley, noting how wet her leg was from me. My hand smelled like her and I couldn't help but sneak another taste.

"Holy fuck," Tenley said, staring up at my ceiling and letting out a little laugh. "That was amazing." She turned her face toward me, eyes bright with wonder.

"You're so fucking cute," I said, kissing her.

She started laughing as I kissed her, so I pulled back. "What is it?"

"Nothing," she said. "I'm just...this night has been a lot." Her laugh turned into a few tears.

"What's wrong, babe?" I said, using my thumb to wipe them away.

"I'm just realizing a lot of things tonight, I'm fine," she said.

I moved closer to her so I could put one arm around her stomach. I also wanted to play with that shiny little gem in her navel. It was really distracting.

"Do you want to talk about it?" I asked, walking my fingers back and forth across her belly.

Tenley shook her head slowly. "No. I don't want to talk. I want you to make me come again."

Now it was my turn to laugh. "I think I can do that," I said, kissing her again.

Chapter Thirteen

"You up for sitting on my face?" I asked.

Tenley nodded as if I'd asked her if she wanted a pony for her birthday. I used pillows and my bedframe to get her in the right position, sitting right on my chest. Tenley looked down at me, her breath coming rapidly.

"You ready?" I asked.

"I'm not going to hurt you?" she asked.

"I'll tap your leg twice if I can't breathe," I said. "How does that sound?"

"Okay," she said, and rose up on her knees, scooting forward a little bit until she was open and glistening for me.

I licked her once, up and down, savoring her, and her body jerked above me and her thighs tensed.

"Oh my *god*," she gasped. "Please do that again."

For a second, I thought about being mean and not doing what she asked, but there would be time for that later. We had all night. If that meant I'd be falling asleep at work, then so be it. I'd take the consequences of these particular actions.

I swirled my tongue around her clit before flicking her entrance, causing her to let out a delicious little whine.

"Fucckkkkkkk," she said, one hand coming down to fist in my hair. Somewhere along the way, my braid had come undone.

Like a woman who had been riding faces forever, she pushed my face closer to where she needed it and if I could have smiled, I would have. At present, my lips and tongue were busy with other tasks.

I pulled from my bag of tricks and worked her over, making my tongue hard and soft and using pressure to gauge what would get her off. Rapid flicks from side to side and hard flat pressure both seemed to do the trick, so I alternated those with licks and plunging my tongue inside her until she was an absolute mess and her nails had probably drawn blood from where they pierced my scalp. At last, I felt her tense and then come completely apart, and it was like being part of an earthquake as she shook and pulsed above me as I did what I could to make her pleasure last as long as possible. Eventually, she made a little sound of pain and her fingers relaxed and let me go. I pushed myself back so I could look up and see her.

Tenley's eyes were bright, and her skin was flushed with the softest pink glow. Her lips formed a smile as she gently gazed down at me.

Tenley let go of my headboard and moved back a little further.

"Can you breathe?" she asked me.

"Sure can," I said, licking her taste from my mouth. "What do you think?"

Tenley nodded a few times. "Yes."

I laughed.

~

"I WANT to take care of you," she said as we lay together a few minutes later. I loved a long sex session. Where there were moments of fire and abandon, followed by moments of supreme stillness, and then the cycle started again.

Tenley sat up with a new intensity in her eyes. She pushed her hair back over her shoulder, tangled and sweaty.

"What should I do?" she asked.

I thought about just having her use her hand like she would on herself, or going down on me, but I also wanted to share my side hustle with her.

"Give me a second," I said, rolling to my unsteady feet and going to the toy box at the foot of the bed. I kept it hidden under a few blankets and pillows so it formed a bench if anyone didn't know what was inside it.

"I'm both scared and intrigued to find out what's in there," Tenley said as I swept off the blankets and unlocked the box. I flung the lid open and searched for one of the first toys I had made, which was still my favorite. It was a green, blue, and purple swirls and fit so perfectly to my anatomy, I had almost cried the first time I'd used it.

"Wanna fuck me with this?" I asked, holding the toy up. It had a flat base so it could be used in a strap-on, but I wasn't sure if Tenley was ready for that on this first night.

Tenley's eyes flicked from the toy to my face and back.

"Hell yeah, I do," she said. "Gimme."

She held her hand out for the toy and I gave it to her, going to get the lube. I was dripping, but I liked the extra slickness of the lube sometimes. I also had some fun lubes that warmed or increased sensation that I used sometimes when I wanted an extra little kick.

I didn't need that tonight. Not with Tenley. We could play with those later.

"It's pretty," she said, stroking the toy.

"Thanks, I made it," I said.

"Wait, you made this?" Tenley asked. Oops. I hadn't meant to blurt that out, but I guess I was telling her now.

"Uh, yeah. Remember when I told you I had a side hustle?" I said, crawling onto the bed with the bottle of lube in one hand. "I make custom silicone sex toys. I happen to be a one-woman quality control team."

Tenley let out a surprised giggle. "So that's why you wouldn't show me the earrings in your jewelry shop."

"I mean, I supposes they could be earrings, but they'd be very heavy and you'd get a lot of strange looks," I said, taking the toy from her and holding it up under my ear. Tenley snorted and took it back from me.

"Get on your back, doll," she said.

Fuck, I loved it when she called me that.

I handed her the bottle of lube and she carefully slicked up the toy, trying different grips until she found what worked.

"I've never fucked anyone before," she said. "I think I'm going to like it." She moved the toy up and down my entrance, hitting my clit and making me gasp. The lube was cold.

"Let's see how you like this," she said, slowly pushing just the tip of the toy inside me. She was so gentle, and she didn't need to be. Tenley could have jammed the entire toy inside me to the hilt and I would have screamed and thanked her at the same time.

I growled in frustration when she removed the toy completely and sat there, holding it up and smirking at me.

"What the fuck, Tenley? You said you wanted to make me come."

"Oh I do. But I also want to play a little bit," she said, moving the toy down and pushing it about halfway in. My body arched toward her, needing more. While the toy wasn't that large, it didn't hit *all* the right spots until it was fully inside me.

"Tenley!" I yelled when she took it out again. She let out a dark laugh and then pushed the toy in again.

"Do you need me to show you how to fuck someone,

because I don't think you're getting it," I said, pushing up on my elbows.

"Were you wanting something more like this?" Tenley asked and then thrust the entire toy inside me with one swift movement, burying it inside me.

"Oh fuck yes, more," I said.

"You got it," Tenley said as she pulled out the toy and then slammed it into me again before doing the same over and over and over.

My knees fell open and I heard myself making all kinds of noises as Tenley fucked me mercilessly with the toy. She wasn't sweet. She wasn't gentle. She was exactly what I needed. Almost.

"Clit, my clit," I said. While I absolutely loved being pounded by a toy, I needed that little extra touch to come.

Tenley paused in her relentless thrusting to figure out the best way to pay attention to my clit while also fucking me with the toy.

"I wish I had a third hand," she said, frustrated when things didn't work out with the right angles.

"I can help with that," I said, sitting up again. "Go into the toy box and find one of the harnesses."

Tenley's eyes widened. "A harness, you say?"

"There's a few in there. You can figure out which one you want. Just hurry." I needed to come so bad I would do just about anything to make it happen.

Tenley hopped off the bed and yanked one of the harnesses over her legs, figuring out how to adjust it in a few moments. I didn't even need to tell her how to insert the toy.

"You look so fucking hot," I said as she climbed onto the bed again, the toy bobbing in the harness.

"I feel fucking hot, I love this," she said, reaching down and stroking the toy.

"Fuck, I could come just from watching you do that," I said, biting back a moan.

"You're not allowed to come until I'm fucking you," Tenley said, angling the toy so it slid inside me, fitting hard with the surge of her hips. I moaned at the intensity and knew that I was so close. So fucking close.

Tenley pulled back and thrust again and it was like she knew exactly what to do by instinct. For her first fuck, she was a master. A prodigy.

Within moments, I was a begging mess and the grin on her face was both feral and beautiful. Her sneaky hand reached between me and the toy as she messily circled my clit and pounded inside me and I completely flew apart into an orgasm so powerful, I didn't know if I would survive its totality. How much pleasure could one body take?

I found out as wave after wave of sharp pleasure shook my entire being as Tenley kept fucking me, wringing me out until I couldn't move.

At last, my body gave out and I lay there flat on my back, unsure if I would ever be able to stand again, or if I would just stay here in this bed, like a decorative moss growing on a rock.

"How are you doing?" Tenley asked and I realized I'd closed my eyes. I levered them open and tilted my head enough so I could look at her. She sat primly with the toy sticking out and with an incredibly smug smile on her face.

"I'll let you know in a few hours," I said, still trying to catch my breath.

"I worked you over that hard? Damn, I'm good at this," she said, stroking the toy again. "I like the way this feels."

"Good," I said. "You can look through my box and see if there's anything you want to try. Every body is different, so you don't know what exactly is going to work until you try it out." That was all part of the fun.

"While writing erotic romances is an amazing job, this is

right up there," she said, pointing at the toy. My brain seemed to be getting some blood back from my lower half and I had an idea that I almost voiced out loud, but I decided it might be better as a surprise. The only thing I'd need to know were Tenley's favorite colors, and if she wanted glitter.

"Go look at some of the toys later. See what you might like. I'll fuck you with it."

"You fuck with a harness too?" she asked.

"Yeah, I'm more of a switch than anything. Depends on my partner," I said.

Tenley sat there and thought about that. If she was writing sapphic erotic books, she obviously knew about tops, bottoms, and switches.

"I don't know what I am," she said. "I mean, I didn't know I had the option."

With a grunt, I shoved myself up and sat closer to her.

"But think about how much fun it's going to be to find out," I said, running my fingers through her tangles. We were both so wrecked and needed showers and sleep. I didn't even want to think about how soon I needed to be awake to get to CG to make lattes and warm up breakfast sandwiches. Far too soon.

Tonight was worth it, though. I'd give up all my sleep for tonight to be witness to Tenley's transformation.

She looked at me through her lashes. "It is going to be fun."

I leaned forward and kissed her. "Come on, let's clean up."

~

TENLEY GRIPED about the quality of the products in my shower, but I shut her up by pushing her against the shower wall and giving her another orgasm with my hand. She retaliated by doing the same and fucking me with those strong typing fingers.

"I think I'm getting the hang of it," she said as she slipped three fingers out of my body and held them up. They were wet, and not from the water coming from the showerhead.

For a second, she stared at them and then licked one finger. Tenley hadn't gone down on me yet, so this was her first taste of me.

"You taste so good," she said, her eyes shutting.

"You sound surprised," I said, trying not to be offended.

"I am," she said, licking each finger in turn. "Pussy is delicious."

I almost choked when she used that word.

"Well," she amended. "Yours is." She kissed me and I wondered how in the hell the two of us had ended up here and how I had gotten this lucky.

The hottest girl in high school thought my pussy was delicious. That was a hell of a thing to share at the next high school reunion, but I was considering it.

Tenley kissed me until I couldn't breathe and then we turned off the water and got out of the shower. I gave her a towel and she grumbled about my brush.

"You should have packed an overnight bag if you wanted all your stuff," I told her as we prepared to brush our teeth in front of the sink. At least I had an unopened spare toothbrush for just such an emergency.

"I didn't know this was going to happen tonight!" she said, taking the toothpaste from me.

"Like I did? I thought you were straight up until a few hours ago," I said.

"Me too!" she yelled and we both laughed in unison.

"Fuck, I have no idea what I'm doing anymore, Mia. This is all very fucking confusing," she said, staring down at her toothbrush.

We both brushed and rinsed and went back to my bedroom so I could give her something to sleep in.

Tenley detangled her hair as I searched through my drawers for something that would work for her, and got pjs for myself too. The bed was pristine since the pad had soaked everything up. I tossed it in the washer and made a note to run that tomorrow when I got back from work.

I did not want to go to work tomorrow. I really wanted to call out. Liam was there to cover anytime, but I still felt a little guilt for not going in due to staying up too late for sex.

Still, I imagined what Lark would tell me. She would absolutely skip work for sex, and I was pretty sure she had. Lark would tell me to go for it, and I knew she'd be proud of me when I told her why I hadn't gone in. I set an alarm on my phone to remind me to get up so I could send an "I'm sick, I can't come in" message to Lark and Liam in the morning so they wouldn't be worried.

"I'm skipping work tomorrow," I said through a yawn when I handed Tenley her pajamas.

"Lucky. I wish I could, but I have to write at least five thousand words," she said.

"How many pages is that?" I asked. I had no idea how many words were in a normal book.

"Too many," she said, pulling my shirt over her head.

"Are you still going to go to Common Grounds?" I asked.

She shook her head and pulled on the shorts I'd given her. "No, it's so much less fun when you're not there. Plus, Lark is going to be staring daggers at me all day and I'd rather keep this between us for now." That made sense.

"If you want, you can go home and get your stuff and work here. I'll probably be sleeping or something," I said. A nice long nap was definitely in my future. There was nothing quite like a good, hard nap.

"That could work," she said. "How about this: we go to my

place and have a nice breakfast and I'll pick you out some books and then we can come back here, and you sleep while I work."

I imagined that scenario in my head. It sounded pretty close to perfect.

"I'll make the lattes," I said.

Tenley grinned and leaned over to kiss me. "I was hoping you'd say that."

Chapter Fourteen

It turned out that Tenley moved around a lot when she slept. I was also pretty sure she had talked a few times in her sleep. I woke up several times when she flipped over or scooted close to me. It wasn't the most restful night, but waking up next to her with her golden hair in my face was priceless.

My alarm went off a few moments later and I sent the message I'd typed out last night to Liam and Lark. He wrote back immediately to tell me to feel better and to not hesitate to take another day if I was still feeling bad. I wasn't going to do that, but it was nice to know that he was supportive of sick days.

"Good morning," Tenley croaked.

"Shhh, it's still really early," I said, putting my phone on silent and setting it aside. "Go back to sleep, babe."

Tenley's eyes were still shut, but a soft smile played on her face.

"I like it when you call me babe," she said. "No one has ever called me that."

I was surprised her ex hadn't, but I had heard him call her "Tens." I wouldn't call her that and remind her of him.

"I like it when you call me 'doll.' No one has called me that before," I said and that made her smile wider and open her eyes.

"Then I get to be first in calling you doll," she said.

"You do," I said, kissing her forehead. "Go back to sleep."

She shut her eyes and a few minutes later she flipped onto her other side and mumbled something I couldn't understand.

~

THE NEXT TIME I AWOKE, Tenley was coming back from the bathroom.

"Hey," she said, getting back into bed and scooting over toward me. I opened my arms and she wiggled into them.

"I've never been the big spoon, I think I might like it," she said, even though she was tucked into my chest.

"You can be the big spoon anytime you want, babe," I said. "But I also reserve the right to big spoon every now and then."

"Deal," she said with a yawn.

"Do you *really* have to write today?" I asked.

She sighed. "I do. I wish I didn't. But I'll type as fast as I can. Even though my fingers are a little tired from last night." She held them up and I brought them to my mouth, biting down softly on the tips.

"I'll give you a hand massage later," I said.

"Ohhh, I like this idea."

Tenley sat up and looked down at me, sleepy and disheveled and so gorgeous it made my heart hurt.

"I don't believe in fate or any of that shit, but I feel like something brought us together," she said.

"I know what you mean," I said, fingering some of her hair. It was all tangled again after she had thrashed in her sleep. "Something about waking up next you feels…inevitable."

"Is inevitable good?" she whispered.

"It's very, very good," I said, slowly kissing her lips.

∽

EVENTUALLY TENLEY and I made it out of bed and headed over to her house. It had taken just about all my willpower not to strip her naked and fuck her senseless until she forgot all about her writing deadline, but I knew how important her career was. After she had finished her work, I could reward her with many orgasms.

"What would you like?" Tenley asked me as she looked into the fridge. I was already working on the coffee situation. She had a milk frother, and the flavored syrups I'd told her to get, so we at least had that.

"I'm fine with whatever. I'm not picky," I said. I really wasn't, when it came to breakfast. It was all good to me. Cheese, bread, eggs, sugar, syrup? Give it to me.

"I'm thinking challah French toast with fruit salad and some crispy potatoes. That work?" Tenley asked me.

"Absolutely," I said. It was way better than the frozen burrito or bagel with cream cheese that I had at home. Or I would have eaten at work and I was so sick of the Common Grounds food that I sometimes made myself go at least a week or two without it.

Tenley turned on some soft music and I got to watch her cook. It reminded me a little of how Lark and I worked so well at Common Grounds when it was busy. Tenley was so comfortable in the kitchen, able to move on instinct.

She was like that with sex too, as I had found out last night.

Little moments kept flooding my brain and I still had a hard time believing it had all happened.

With a start, I brought myself back to the present and out

of the memory of Tenley fucking me with my own toy. New sex fantasy: unlocked.

Once she was done with work, I was going to fulfill another new fantasy: finding out which one of my toys made her scream the most so I could pour a special one just for her. Tenley's birthday was in February, but that didn't mean I couldn't give her an extremely belated present.

Tenley buzzed around the kitchen as I made lattes for both of us, handing one to her as she flipped the French toast. She took a sip and closed her eyes in bliss.

"It's always better when you make it," she said.

"Thanks," I said.

Since the weather was so nice, I suggested eating outside, but Tenley made a face.

"There are ticks out there and I haven't had a chance to get the grass cut in a while," she said. "I feel like I get so focused on writing that I forget to go outside for more than a few minutes. That's probably bad, isn't it?"

I pulled her into a hug, kissing her cheek. "We'll work on it. One step at a time. We'll eat in the living room with the windows open."

Tenley chuckled. "That's a good first step."

~

BREAKFAST WAS phenomenal and I had to stop myself from eating too fast. The sooner we got back to my place, the sooner Tenley could get her work done, and the sooner I could be fucking her senseless. That was my ultimate goal today, other than a satisfying nap.

Once the dishes were taken care of and Tenley packed up her stuff, including an overnight bag that I didn't comment on, and a few paperbacks for me, we went back to my place.

"Let me know what you need," I said as she pulled out her laptop and sat on the couch with her legs stretched out.

"Yeah, this will work," she said, nodding and standing up again. "I just need some water, I think. I set timers to remind me to take breaks. This will probably take me about three hours? Four? Hopefully. If everyone cooperates." She went to the kitchen to get some water and I couldn't help but be fascinated by how her creative mind worked.

"I'm going to try and take a nap, but please don't hesitate if you need something. You can message me," I said, holding up my phone.

"I'm a big girl, I can handle it, but thank you," Tenley said, giving me a quick kiss. "Enjoy your nap, doll."

She sat down on the couch with her laptop and put her headphones on, and I wished I could watch her like I did every day at the coffee shop. Instead, I went to my room and shut the door, almost all the way. Within a few moments, I was completely and totally asleep.

∽

I DIDN'T WAKE up until there was a warm body pressed against me and lips on my forehead. My brain floated back to consciousness and I realized Tenley had gotten into bed with me.

"I'm finished with work," she said, and my eyes opened.

"What time is it?" I asked.

"Early afternoon. I was going to make some lunch for us, are you hungry?" She pushed my hair back from my face.

"Yeah, sure. You can use whatever is in there," I said. Maybe I should jump out of bed and cook for her, but she was better at it than I was and we'd both enjoy her food more anyway.

"Perfect," she said, but she didn't get up immediately.

"How were the words?" I asked.

"Slow, but I think most of them are salvageable," she said with a little laugh.

"I'm sure they're much better than that," I said. "Would you let me read some?"

Tenley pressed her lips together. "I don't know about that. No one sees my first drafts but me. I don't hand them off to my editor until they're as clean as I can get them."

"You don't have to," I said.

"I'll think about it." She kissed me again and then slipped out of bed to go make lunch.

∽

I WAS BACK to my usual self after the nap and eating the sandwiches and salad that Tenley had cobbled together from what I had in the apartment.

"You up for getting fucked?" I asked Tenley as we lazed together on the couch. Her laptop was packed away and she was all mine for the rest of the day.

She turned her face and met my gaze.

"Yes, please," she said, kissing me.

"Give me just a few minutes to set up," I said, getting to my feet.

∽

BY THE TIME I called Tenley into the bedroom, I had a bunch of toys laid out, a new pad on the bed, and my harness ready to go. Sex prep was so important.

Tenley's eyes widened as she looked at all the toys spread out on my bed. They were all vibrant colors and interesting shapes, with a few classics in there too.

"There's so many of them," she breathed.

"The best way to narrow it down is to get rid of the ones you are absolutely sure you don't want to use, and then go from there," I said.

Tenley tilted her head to the side in the most adorable way as she studied the toys, reaching for each one, picking it up and giving it a good look.

The process took a while, and I was pleased by how seriously she took the selection process. Finally, she had the collection narrowed down to three toys. One had bulbous ridges, another had small bumps all over its curved surface, and the third was shaped very much like a classic toy.

"Satisfied?" I asked.

"Not yet," she said, kissing my cheek and then pulling off her clothes. I hurried to do the same before yanking the harness on and making sure the straps were adjusted and in the right place. Just putting it on got me wet.

I got the lube ready and asked Tenley which one she wanted to start with. She picked the classic shape.

"If none of these work, we can try more. We can try them all," I said.

She laughed. "I don't know if that idea is scary or the hottest thing I've ever heard."

"Both?" I asked as I fitted the toy into the harness and made sure it was secure before slicking it with lube.

"I don't need any foreplay, I'm ready," Tenley said, spreading her legs. "It was almost impossible to think about my characters fucking when all I could think about was this."

"I had quite a few naked dreams about you during my nap," I said as I positioned myself over her, reveling in how our bodies fit together.

"And how does reality stack up with those dreams?" she asked just before I slid inside her.

"Better," I said, burying the entirety of the toy inside her, making her gasp. "This is so much better."

I fucked her slowly at first, but with a hard slam at the very end that she seemed to like. If I wanted, I could probably fuck her right off this bed and onto the floor and she'd beg me to go harder.

"Harder," she said, as if she had read my mind.

"You got it, babe," I said, thrusting into her with greater force. Tenley arched into me and moaned, and she was so beautiful that she didn't seem real.

"Red light," Tenley said, and I immediately stopped.

"You okay?" I asked. I hoped I hadn't hurt her.

"Yeah, this just isn't working for me. It's not enough. Can we try another?" she asked, panting. Her face was tight with concentration, and I knew she was trying to reach for a climax that was just out of reach and she needed to find the exact right combination that would shove her over the edge.

"Of course," I said, pulling out and removing the toy. I held up the other two.

"That one," she said, selecting the toy with all the tiny bumps on it. Something told me that might be the one she wanted. I put it in the harness and just added a little lube to smooth the way. I worked the tip of the toy up and down her entrance, seeing how she responded to the bumps.

"Ohhhh," she said, her eyes fluttering closed. "That's good."

This time I thrust inside her slowly, so she could feel every single inch.

"Oh, *Mia*," she moaned, and I knew we had a winner.

The key with this toy was to fuck smarter, not harder. With all the different textures on it, a little more finesse was required, so I rolled my hips with every thrust until she was practically sobbing as she begged me to let her come. Because I wasn't a monster, I moved one hand between us to stroke her clit and she finally came, her body convulsing so hard she shook the whole bed. She screamed, and I hoped all of my neighbors were at work and didn't hear her. Or maybe I wanted them to. Wanted them to hear what I was responsible for.

Tenley's orgasm went on and I brought her through it and to the other side until her body stilled and she looked up at me.

"I like that one," she said, and I snorted.

"Yeah, I can tell," I said, shaking with my own need above her. Tenley must have seen the strain on my face because she reached between us and snuck her clever fingers between the toy and my center, stroking my clit.

"Oh, fuck," I said, my arms trembling as I tried to hold myself up and she pushed me toward my own climax.

"That's my girl. Come for me. Let me see it on your pretty face," she said and that was it. Her words set off my orgasm and I collapsed on top of her as the waves pulled me under. She held me and kissed my face until the storm quieted and I was warm and sleepy again.

I rolled onto my back next to her, still wearing the toy.

"I definitely think you should skip work more often," she said, flicking her fingers against the toy and making it wobble.

"I'd quit my job if we got to do this every day," I said, still breathing heavy.

"And what would you do for money?" she asked.

I flipped onto my side so I could stare at her. The toy brushed against her leg, leaving a trail.

"Mooch off my author girlfriend?" I asked and Tenley gave a start at that last word.

"Oh, am I your girlfriend now? You've just decided that?" she asked, but there was a smile in her voice.

"I mean, you were the one who asked me to be your fake girlfriend. I'm asking you to be my real one," I said. "What do you think?"

Tenley grinned and my heart hammered in my chest in excitement.

"I already came out, so I don't have to do that again. I

mean, I still don't know where the hell I fall on whatever sexuality scale there is," she said.

"It's okay," I said, kissing the tip of her nose. "We can figure it out together. Will you be my girlfriend?"

Tenley nodded and let out a giggle. "I think I'm going to like being your real girlfriend."

Chapter Fifteen

HAVING Tenley as my real girlfriend was so much easier than having a fake girlfriend. She slid absolutely seamlessly into my life and within a week, it was like we'd always been dating. For someone who'd only ever had one boyfriend, Tenley was an excellent girlfriend. During one of my breaks at work when a customer had made me cry (before Liam threw him out), she'd gone out and come back with a massive box of beautiful cupcakes, all the way from Sweet's in Castleton.

"You're going to share those, right?" Lark asked, peering into the box when Tenley presented it to me.

"Maybe," I said, drawing out the word. "Maybe I'll share."

"I'll remind you how many times I have fed you, Mia," Lark said.

I rolled my eyes. "Okay fine, you can have two."

"Sydney will be upset if I don't get her one," Lark pointed out.

"You can have three," I amended.

Tenley also wanted to meet my sister and my niece much sooner than I would have expected.

"They're important to you," she said. "And you talk about

them all the time, so I feel like I'm missing out. I'd introduce you to my brothers, but they're animals."

"I've met your brothers," I said. "I don't care to repeat the experience."

"That's fine, you can avoid them. I do."

It was Tenley's suggestion that we pick up dinner and bring it over to Ingrid's house so she wouldn't have to cook or wash dishes, which was so thoughtful that I had to make out with her in the car before we went in.

Ingrid had been shocked when I informed her that my former fake girlfriend was not, in fact, straight and now she was my real girlfriend, but she'd kept the judgment to a minimum.

"Hey, Miss Athena," I said when I walked in the door and almost crashed into my niece, who was doing laps around the couch.

"Hi hi," Athena said, still doing her zoomies. I had no idea what well of energy toddlers drew from, but I wanted some of that.

"Athena, can you stop for a minute? I want to introduce you to someone." Tenley carried the pizza box and the bags with appetizers and salads from Nick's Pizza, which was the main restaurant in Arrowbridge, and also happened to be the best.

Athena put on her brakes and skidded to a stop in front of me, seeing Tenley for the first time. Her little eyes went wide as I took the food from Tenley.

She crouched down to Athena's level. "Hi, I'm Tenley. It's nice to meet you, Athena."

"Tenny," Athena said. Close enough.

"You can call me Tenny if you want," Tenley said. "It can be a hard name to say."

Confident that Tenley had Athena in her thrall, I went to

the kitchen to set the bags down as Ingrid came out from the bathroom, her eyes wide.

"Oh, I thought I heard you come in. I had to pee so bad and I was hoping my little monster didn't destroy the house," she said. Ingrid looked exhausted. Even more so than usual. Her tired face made a pang of guilt go through me. I needed to step up more and help out. She was doing this whole thing alone and it was impossible. Fucking impossible.

"This smells amazing," Ingrid said, popping open the pizza box.

"Yeah, you can't miss with Nick's."

Ingrid looked over where Tenley and Athena were chatting as if they were bffs and snorted. "Looks like your girlfriend has already charmed my daughter."

I couldn't hide my smile as Tenley looked up at me and winked. "Looks like she did."

∽

INGRID PULLED me aside after we'd devoured the pizza and Athena had only had one small toddler moment before demanding that Tenley look at all her toys and then sit on the couch to watch cartoons with her. Tenley didn't object at all and seemed enchanted by Athena and somehow knew all the names of the characters and had already seen Athena's favorite movies.

"She's a witch," Ingrid said, shaking her head as we talked in the kitchen. I wanted to know what she thought about Tenley, but I was afraid to ask.

"Not quite. Just one of those people that everyone loves," I said. "She is kind of magic, though."

Ingrid nodded. "I can't make a full assessment after one dinner, but I take my daughter's opinion very highly and I'm pretty sure Athena is about to ask her to move in with us, so that tips everything way over in Tenley's favor."

She pulled me in for a hug and sighed. "She's great, Mia, you know that. You don't need my approval."

"I know. But I like having it anyway," I said as Athena babbled something to Tenley and she talked right back, making Athena laugh.

"You've got it," she said, releasing me from the hug.

∼

ATHENA NEEDED to go to bed soon after and insisted that Tenley come with her. Tenley laughed and went with her. I headed out to the garage to fiddle around with my equipment. Part of me was still a little apprehensive about showing her this part of me, but two days ago she'd let me read some of her unedited work (which was flawless, as far as I could see), and now it was my turn to reveal myself.

I did a quick inventory of my colors, making notes of what I was low on so I could place an order before I ran out.

"So this is your secret space," Tenley said, and I looked up to find her hovering in the doorway between the house and the garage.

"This is it. My humble workshop where I produce my bespoke toys," I said as she came toward me. Tenley wandered around, looking at everything, including the shelves that had toys on them.

"You know I've been thinking, about that one toy I like so much. I think it could be improved if you added bubbles like this," she said, picking up a toy that was ridged.

"I can do that," I said. My plan to make her a custom toy was still in the works in my head. "If I did make one, what colors should I use?" I gestured to my selection.

Tenley skipped over and looked through them all.

"Pink and purple," she finally said. "Swirly. With glitter."

Somehow, I had a feeling those would be her choices. Tenley loved lots of bright colors, but she had a special affinity for pink.

"I'll see what I can do," I said.

"You'd make it for me?" she asked.

I huffed out a breath. "Yes, I was planning to surprise you, but you just ruined it."

Tenley let out a delighted laugh and threw her arms around me.

"You're the best girlfriend ever," she said, smacking a kiss on my cheek as she rocked us back and forth. Her exuberance was contagious.

"I don't know about that. You're pretty great at it," I said, pulling back so I could gaze into her face. She was so beautiful and so fun and so sweet and she was all mine.

"I didn't know I could be a good girlfriend until someone showed me how," she said. "I mean you, in case you were wondering."

I snorted. "Yeah, I assumed it was me." Shane couldn't teach someone to find their way out of a paper bag. Tenley had opened up more about their relationship and told me that when we'd been fake dating, Shane had demanded that we join him for a threesome. He was a complete and utter pig, and if I saw him at the grocery store, I was going to throw a can of soup at him or something.

Tenley had been right that most of her friends had "chosen" to stay friends with Shane and her invites to barn parties had dried up. That just meant I had swept her into my group, and I could tell she was a whole lot happier. Being around kind people who weren't judgmental bores with nothing interesting to say was doing wonders for her social life. Then there was Karissa, who had come to hang out with us a few times and visited Common Grounds a few times a week to get coffee and chat. It was nice to have yet another new person in my orbit, and Tenley and I were working on getting her to join book club.

Life with Tenley was bright and happy and full of laughs and sex and cupcakes and books and I was so fucking grateful that I'd gotten over that high school bullshit and seen her for the wonderful person that she was. If I hadn't, I would have missed out on everything.

Tenley was everything and she was *mine*.

"Let's go to my house," she said, keeping her hand in mine as we went back into the house to say goodnight to Ingrid.

"Why yours?" I asked. "Mine has all the fun stuff." I wiggled my eyebrows so she would know what I meant.

"Yes, but mine has all the books," she said in my ear before nipping at my earlobe.

"What could be better than sex and books?" I asked her in a whisper. There were always little ears listening in this house, so you had to be careful what you said at a normal volume.

"You," Tenley said, placing a soft kiss on my mouth. "You're the best out of all of them."

"No, I think that's you," I said back, and we argued all the way to my apartment to grab the sex toys we'd need for the evening before going back over to Tenley's.

We eventually agreed to disagree.

Epilogue

"I'm nervous!" Tenley said as we sat together staring at her laptop screen. Her latest sapphic erotic romance was ready to publish, and all she had to do was press the button to send it to the online retailers, but she was dragging her feet. This was the second time she'd done this while we'd been together and I got the feeling she had a little breakdown every single time, even though she'd done this before.

It was adorable.

"Do you want me to do it?" I asked as she gnawed at her lip.

"No, I can do it," she said. "I just…what if I screwed it all up? What if it's completely unreadable? What if they all hate it?" She dropped her head into her hands and let out a wail.

"They're not going to hate it. Your readers love your work. They tell you all the time. You've been through edits. Your editor is a professional that you pay to make sure your books are the best they can be. Tenley, you are an incredible author. Just do it."

I lifted her face so she could look into my eyes and see the truth there.

"You're so fucking talented it scares me," I said, kissing her. "Now hit the button and I'll fuck you with your favorite toy as a reward."

She slammed the pad on her keyboard and a message came up that her book was in process and would be live soon.

Tenley let out a shaky breath. "Fuck, that never gets easier." She pushed away from the table and stood up, pacing around her office.

As much as I loved my little apartment, Tenley's house was bigger and nicer, so we spent the majority of our time here. I'd been a little reluctant to give up my place, but my lease was up in two months, and I would be officially moving in with Tenley. She had already given me the run of the entire basement to expand my toy business, which was booming, thanks to the new space, and thanks to my second product tester. Tenley had excellent instincts about toys, and even helped me package everything up on weekends when she didn't have a writing deadline.

She still came to Common Grounds every day and she'd started harassing me for free drinks again, but I just smiled and gave her free ones, because I'd signed her up for the Coffee Club membership.

"Come on, my bestselling author girlfriend. It's time to turn your brain off for a little while," I said, pushing her through the door and down the hall to her bedroom.

Tenley pushed me toward the bed, kissing me and pulling at my clothes as we went.

"I want to turn my brain off by fucking you first until you scream my name," she said, shoving me so I fell back onto the mattress.

"I love it when you're all toppy," I said. Over the months, Tenley had settled on bisexual for her label, with the option of changing it at any time. It didn't matter to me. I just wanted to be with her and love her and build a life together.

"You love me when I'm bottomy too," she said, flinging open the toy box so she could select her tools.

"Probably because I just love you," I said as she held up my new favorite toy that we had designed together. I watched as she expertly stepped into the harness and added the toy before adding just a little lube.

Tenley kissed me and gazed down at me for a moment before fitting the toy to my entrance.

"And I love you," she said as she thrust inside me. "I love you, Mia."

I was unable to respond with anything other than moaning her name.

∽

STAY TUNED for Charmed By Her (Mainely Books 6), an unlikely romance between Karissa, who can't wait to get out of Arrowbridge, and Ingrid, who only wants to take care of her family. Turn the page for a teaser!

About Charmed By Her

The only thing I had to look forward to was getting as far away from my hometown of Arrowbridge, Maine, as possible. That is, until I bump into a single mom and her bug-loving daughter. Ingrid Davidson and I have absolutely nothing in common. She's older, she has a child, and she's settled in Arrowbridge for good.

Still, I can't stop finding reasons to spend time with her, and her adorable toddler. There's no rule that I can't have a friend before I head off to my new life. Just one small problem: my feelings for Ingrid are not just friendly.

Not only is she unbelievably stunning, but she's funny and I love the way she is with her daughter. Ingrid's life as a single mom isn't easy, and the pull to want to be there for her is undeniable. As my original plans start to fade further into the background, I wonder if I could make a good life in Arrowbridge, or if I have to follow my plans to get away once and for all.

∼

"Athena!" a sharp voice said as I headed across the parking lot that separated the bank I worked at from Common Grounds Coffee Shop. I turned and quickly saw a little redheaded girl booking it across the lot as fast as her little legs would carry her. Without even thinking, I sprinted for her and snatched her up, just as a car was backing up. I moved away from the car, making sure to hold tight to the wiggling girl.

"Stay still," I told her, but that didn't seem to have an effect on her. Once I had her safely on one of the grass medians, I set her down.

"Athena, oh my god!" A woman swept the girl up in her arms, clinging to her.

"Mama, mama," the little girl said, so I was going to take a wild guess and say this was her mom.

"Oh my god, don't ever do that to me again," the woman said, still clutching her daughter with tears streaming down her face. She didn't seem to be aware I was there and I wondered if I should just leave them alone to have their moment.

The mom took a deep breath and then set the little girl down, but kept hold of one of her hands.

"Look at me, Athena," the mom said, her voice switching to a stern tone that made me stand up straight and hope that there were no stains on my shirt.

"Remember how we talked about parking lots? That you need to stay very close to mama because there are lots of people and cars that can't see you?"

The little girl nodded and then started to cry.

"Oh, baby, it's okay. I just want you to be safe. That's all I want," the mom said, giving her daughter a hug and soothing her sobs.

She looked up and saw me for the first time.

"I'm so sorry, thank you for grabbing her. She's normally so good, but we all have our moments. Learning the rules of the world is a process." She gave me a soft smile and I was slammed in the stomach with instant attraction. I wasn't sure of her age, but she was definitely a few years older than my twenty-three years, with medium brown hair that was pulled back from her face with a tortoiseshell clip. It was her eyes, though, that I really noticed. They weren't quite blue and they weren't quite green. Some mixture of two that in the sunlight made me think of the ocean in the summer. Beautiful.

"You're welcome," I said. "I'm just glad I was in the right place at the right time."

The mom stood up and studied me for a moment. "You look familiar. Are you from Arrowbridge?" Her stunning eyes narrowed, as if she was trying to place me.

"Uh, yeah. I grew up here. I'm Karissa Ballencourt," I said, holding out my hand.

"Ingrid Davidson," she said, and then I realized I knew who she was too. Mia Davidson had been in my graduating class and this must be her older sister. That meant she was definitely older than me, by at least five years, and she had a daughter.

We lived completely different lives.

The two of us stood there in silence until the little girl tugged on her mother's arm.

"Mama, you didn't introduce me," she said, glaring in only the way a disgruntled toddler can. I tried to hide a smile.

"Oh my goodness, I'm sorry. This is Athena," she said, pulling Athena in front of her.

"Hi, Athena. That's a very special name you have," I said, crouching down. She was an adorable little thing, with wild red hair and blue eyes.

Athena put her hand out like her mother had. I shook it gently.

"A pessure to meet you," she said, and I had to swallow a laugh. I looked up at her mom and we shared a smile.

"It's a pleasure to meet you too," I said. My break was over in a few minutes and if I didn't hurry, I wasn't going to get my caffeine fix.

"We should probably get going. We're headed to the d-o-c-t-o-r," she said, lowering her voice.

Athena glared up at her mother suspiciously.

"We just came by to say hi to Auntie Mia and get a treat," Ingrid said as Athena started clapping her little hands around one of Ingrid's.

"I'm headed over there myself," I said, not sure why I was stalling.

"I hope you enjoy yourself and tell Mia that whatever you order is on me," she said.

"Oh, that's not necessary," I said, but she put her hand on my arm.

"You saved my daughter. I owe you more than a coffee," she said, and I felt my face going red. I just did what anyone else would have. Well, anyone who wasn't a serial killer or something.

"It was no problem," I said, shifting in my work shoes. I couldn't wait to slip them off when I got home.

"Mama," Athena said, tugging at her mother's arm. "We late!"

Ingrid checked her phone and I heard her curse softly under her breath. "She's right, we are going to be late." She met my gaze with those incredible eyes, and it was like diving into a pool.

"Listen, I want to do something to thank you. I don't know what that is right now, but something. Tell Mia your number and I'll reach out," she said, and I wanted to protest that it wasn't necessary at all, but something made me stop.

I wanted to see her again. The truth of it hammered in my chest and stole my breath.

I absolutely needed to see her again.

Reading List

A Game of Hearts and Heists by Ruby Roe (Chapter 3)
Don't Stop Me by Eden Emory (Chapter 4)
No Strings Attached by Harper Bliss (Chapter 4)
The Fate of Stars by SD Simper (Chapter 7)

About the Author

Chelsea M. Cameron is a New York Times/USA Today/Internationally Best Selling author from Maine who now lives and works in Boston. She's a red velvet cake enthusiast, obsessive tea drinker, former cheerleader, and world's worst video gamer. When not writing, she enjoys watching infomercials, eating brunch in bed, tweeting, and playing fetch with her cat, Sassenach. She has a degree in journalism from the University of Maine, Orono that she promptly abandoned to write about the people in her own head. More often than not, these people turn out to be just as weird as she is.

Connect with her on Twitter, Facebook, Instagram, Bookbub, Goodreads, and her Website.

If you liked this book, please take a few moments to **leave a review**. Authors really appreciate this and it helps new readers find books they might enjoy. Thank you!

Also by Chelsea M. Cameron

The Noctalis Chronicles
Fall and Rise Series
My Favorite Mistake Series
The Surrender Saga
Rules of Love Series
UnWritten
Behind Your Back Series
OTP Series
Brooks (The Benson Brothers)
The Violet Hill Series
Unveiled Attraction
Anyone but You
Didn't Stay in Vegas
Wicked Sweet
Christmas Inn Maine
Bring Her On
The Girl Next Door
Who We Could Be
Castleton Hearts
Mainely Books Club

Allured By Her is a work of fiction. Names, characters, places and incidents are either the product of the author's imagination or are use fictitiously. Any resemblance to actual persons, living or dead, events, business establishments or locales is entirely coincidental.

No part of this book may be reproduced, scanned or distributed in any printed or electronic form without permission. All rights reserved.

Copyright © 2023 Chelsea M. Cameron

Editing by Laura Helseth

Cover by Chelsea M. Cameron

Printed in Great Britain
by Amazon